Tanyania,
Thank you so
for your support.
love the series as much

True North

Fight The Void

S.M. Winter

S.M. Winter

S.M. Winter Publication

Ordering Information:
Quantity sales. Special discounts are available on quantity purchases by corporations, associations, and others. For details, contact the publisher at the address above.
eBook version available at all major electronic retailers.

Printed in the US

Table of Contents

Acknowledgements

First, I want to thank my best friend and sister, Aimee. Without her support I would not have been able to finish this book as quickly as I did. She is also my editor and artisan behind the physical Elemental Keys.

I would also like to thank my husband Andrew and my Beta Readers, who gave no holds-barred feedback, even if it did crush my hopes and dreams. I love you all, thank you for your frightening honesty. Especially my husband Andrew who read and reread every version I was working on. Also a big thanks to Kane and his wife Crystal who helped further edit the book in a short amount of time. You two are beautiful, stay classy.

Lastly I would like to thank everyone who turned out in support when I started my Facebook page and helped me announce my impending book release. You all have been so amazing! I'm excited to see what you think of the finished product and look forward to the next.

 Hesitating, I watched as the cars sped past the road before me. I fantasized about stepping out in front of one of them. Turning away from the road I watched as people walked quickly by, each one a blur as they passed. First one foot, then the other slipped backward so that all that held me to the curb was the balls of my feet. My heart pounded in my chest, fluttering like a caged bird who knew its time was near. Shaking the bars as if it could change its fate. I scoffed at the bird. This was how it needed to end. All I needed was the nerve to take that last step.

As I hung there, waiting to drum up that last bit of courage I watched as people passed, oblivious to my struggle. I closed my eyes and listened to the vehicles speed by behind me. The wind from the departures was blowing up the back of my shirt making it float in their false zephyrs. As I raised my arms and took a deep breath I started to lean backward. Then I caught myself. What was I doing? There were people who needed me. I couldn't leave them like this. It was selfish. A smile broke out over my face as I realized something important: *I didn't want to die.* Unfortunately, that was the exact moment my choice was taken from me.

Before I could even open my eyes, I heard a jostling in front of me and I was pushed. My lack of balance left me without a hand or foot hold and I fell backward. The bird in my chest shook the bars so hard I could barely catch my breath to scream. As my eyes flew open I saw someone standing before me, smiling. Then they vanished in a literal puff of smoke before I hit the ground. My impromptu flight seemed to slow as I neared the ground. The world around me came to a crawl, then stopped altogether. When I hit the ground I expected everything to start again. I expected honks and severe pain from being hit by the car that was literally two inches from my head. But this was different. This wasn't that moment before death where everything stands still and your life flashes before your eyes. Everything around me was frozen in time.

I stood up quickly and moved out of the way, back to the safety of the sidewalk and looked around. People and vehicles alike were still as early morning lake water. It called to mind a movie scene that had been moving quickly, but someone hit the pause button. There were even movement lines, a slight blurring that implied they had been moving quickly. It was because this dead silence and lack of movement that I heard the quick footsteps leading away from the street.

Following the noise, I left the frightening scene behind me and walked down the nearest alley, where the footsteps seemed to be echoing. As I left the street movement resumed and the noise came screaming back making it harder to follow the retreating footsteps.

"Wait!" I called into the hazy darkness of the alley as I raced in pursuit, of what I had no clue. All I knew was that they must have answers.

I ran to the end of the alley. However, instead of a person, I found a wall. Solid and brick, it stood there mocking me. I wanted to yell. I wanted to rage and release my frustration. My hands shook so I gripped them tight into fists, squeezed my eyes shut and breathed deep. The fetid stench of the alley greeted me and I instantly regretted my decision to breath. My eyes popped open as I choked on my tongue, and after a few hacking coughs to clear my lungs, began breathing through my teeth. Something clean and white lying on the ground amidst the grime of the alley caught my attention. As I bent down to pick it up, it began to burn from the edges. A small white business card with three little words printed on it:

I've Been Waiting

I watched as the card erupted into small flames and puffed into invisibility. I coughed again at the smoke it left behind, waving my hand in front of my face to clear my view of the area. Exactly in the spot the card had been was a single flower. A dandelion, growing from a newly formed crack in the asphalt.

Confused but reluctantly charmed, I looked around and found the alley as empty as it had been when I'd entered it. Picking up a discarded soup can I bent and dug around the crack and gently dislodging the tiny weed, filled the can. It seemed wrong to just leave it in the darkness to die all alone.

Taking my prize I walked to the mouth of the alley, contemplating what had just transpired in the last few minutes. All I knew for sure was that I must be having some sort of mental break and more importantly, that I wanted to live. Sighing, I held my tiny miserable flower close and stepped into the hustle and bustle of the New York City streets.

As I entered the hospital, my hands clutched reflexively around the tiny plant. I swear I could almost feel the plant lean toward me in support. This time when I took a deep breath I was greeted with the burning smell and taste of antiseptic. Just as jarring, but less natural, than the stench from the alley. At least in the alley I knew I was smelling the decay that surrounded me. In a hospital the decay lurked under the uniform chemical scent. I've found that all hospitals smell nearly identical. The metallic scent of death and decay under the shine. I shivered as I entered the waiting room and allowed the heavy burden of what lay before me settle back onto my shoulders.

The small escape I'd allowed myself dissolved, along with the theory that I could take control and make this waking nightmare end. So I gathered the small amount of courage I had left and walked to room 312. Before I could enter a rough hand grabbed my shoulder, whipping me around.

"Where have you been?" Demanded the woman before me.

She stood nearly a twelve inches shorter than my five foot six. I could see the small bald spot at the crown of her head, hair that she usually kept quaffed perfectly to hide the flaw, hung in lank resignation. It was a testament to her distraction and emotional state that she would go out in public imperfect. Dark circles drew her eyes inward making them look hollow and sunken. She still had makeup on, but it was smeared as if she'd rubbed her eyes too deeply. The expression that settled onto her face, upon confronting me, was that of bored derision. A look I'd seen from one of the earliest memories I had as a child.

"Hello mother," my voice devoid of emotion; I knew how she could turn vicious if she so much as scented weakness.

"Don't hello mother me," she spat. "I asked you a question."

"I..." Looking around I searched for an excuse. Telling the truth was simply not an option unless I wanted to be locked up for the rest of my life. I knew she would throw me to the wolves without a thought. I, after all, was not her favorite. Her favorite sat in room 312. My hands clenched involuntarily again around the can I held, reminding me that it still sat in my hands.

"I went to get her flowers," I replied lamely, my voice quiet and subdued.

"That?" The woman who called herself my mother scoffed. "That is a weed, it goes in the garbage."

She ripped the tiny plant in its temporary home from my hands and tossed it unceremoniously into the nearest refuse bin. I shuddered with the plant as it connected with the bottom.

"Go back out and get something that is worthy of your sister's death," she sniffed.

"Is she..." My eyes welled at the thought of my sister passing on while I was out selfishly considering my own end.

"No, stupid girl," the glint in her eyes telling me she'd caught the scent and relished the hunt. "You haven't killed her yet. She's hanging on by a thread, so you better hurry. She will die and soon. Buy her something with your fancy money from your fancy job."

Appropriately shamed, as she wanted, I turned and walked dutifully to the nearest gift shop. As soon as I felt her burning gaze fall from my retreating form, I let the tears fall. I refuse to let her see me cry again.

"Here." A tissue was shoved into my hand by a tiny blonde in a candy stripers uniform.

"Thank you," I choked out as I rubbed it across my eyes.

"No problem," she smiled and winked. "I carry them in my pockets for this exact reason. Part of the job."

I gave a watery laugh and she moved on down the hall. Patting shoulders and lending tissues where needed. She must be a saint to comfort people for a living. Balling up the used tissues, I threw them in a small trash bin nearby and moved to the display of flowers. There was a wide selection from elaborate bouquets to small and simple ones. I know my sister would be happy with something small, but my mother would surely turn up her snobby nose at it, saying I was trying to be cheap.

I graduated from Yale at 16 just a few years ago. I majored in Art History and Design specializing in Museum Operations. It's something that I should be proud of, but instead it's a point of scorn for my mother. Before I finished school I was recruited for an internship at the American Museum of Natural History in New York. My sister ended up going to NYU so we lived together for a year while she was studying. Though she was five years older than me, I graduated High School at twelve-years-old, which was a full year ahead of her. While I interned, I continued my education and just this year finished my PhD in Preservation Studies.

My sister was thrilled when I finished my Doctorate. We learned not to tell our mother about my accomplishments. When my sister graduated from NYU, a year into my PhD, our mother threw her a block party in our old neighborhood. Naturally, I wasn't invited. Everyone from our neighborhood thought that I had dropped out of school and run away at fifteen, so I wasn't insulted. I was happy for my sister.

They married after she turned nineteen. Only one year into college, which was too young in my opinion, but some would say the same about a nineteen-year-old getting their Doctorate. It's been five years since their wedding day and she threw me a surprise party to celebrate my Doctorate. She'd gotten me to come by saying it was their five year anniversary party. So I went. Imagine my surprise when I walked in and everyone cheered, not for her but for me. There were people I hadn't seen in years, and a lot of my work associates. I didn't make friends easily so it was nice to see some familiar faces. It was hard to believe that this transpired just a few days ago. It felt like it had been years. I squeezed my eyes shut as I relived the horror.

The party was going well and I was overwhelmed with love and gratitude for my sister. Even if some of the attendees looked awkward to be there, I was happy that she had gone to the trouble to guilt or badger people to come. When the party ran out of ice I volunteered to get some, but she wouldn't hear of it. She grabbed her keys, winked at me and said she'd be right back. That was three days ago.

That had been the last thing she'd said to me. On her way to the corner market, just a few minutes' walk down the street, she'd been hit by a truck. The driver had lost control, spun off the road and pinned her between the wall of a building and the hood. What made it even worse was that the truck had driven off and left her to die alone on the sidewalk.

Her impending death is my fault. The doctors have no hope. She had no pulse for more than ten minutes while they rushed her to the hospital. They were able to get her heart started again, but the damage was done. Her body cannot function on its own so she will be hooked up to machines for the rest of her life. The doctors have suggested we withdraw care. My mother would keep her on the machines indefinitely, so it's a good thing her husband has the power of attorney. He decided to wait 72 hours to give the family time to say goodbye. I've barely left the hospital in that time. Shaking my head to clear it I concentrated on the task at hand.

Flowers. Choosing the largest bouquet they carried, I paid and walked to the cafeteria. Seeing Jonathan, my sister's husband, with their two children I sat down with them at the table and watched as he tried to beg his three and four year old to eat. My nephews looked at the food solemnly. Tad, the three-year-old, clutched his stuffed elephant and clamped his mouth shut as his father tried to shove food inside. Groaning in frustration he dropped the fork and shoved both his hands through his already mussed hair.

"I want mommy," Tad's bottom lip quivered as he looked at me. "Is she awake yet?"

"No honey," I replied. "I'm sorry."

Thomas, the four-year-old, regarded me oddly but didn't make a sound.

"I can take it from here Jon, if you need a break," I told him.

"That would be great," he sighed. "I just need a couple minutes. I'll be right back boys."

The boys watched as he walked away without commenting. When he went out of sight their attention was on me. I felt slightly unsettled by their stares.

"So..." I said. "Why don't you want to eat?"

Tad walked around the table and crawled into my lap, snuggling close, silently playing with his elephant.

"It's stinky," Thomas replied. His lower lip was poking out as he surveyed his younger brother's position, as if he envied the occupation of my lap.

"Stinky huh?" I looked at the macaroni and cheese and jello sitting on the table.

I grabbed a fork and popped a bite into my mouth. The cheese was rubbery and nearly glued the inside of my mouth shut. I coughed lightly and eyed the gelatin as it seemed to shimmy of its own volition.

"I see what you mean," I said.

Thomas watched me with interest, but not a glimmer of the smile I'd hoped to achieve.

"Hmm," I thought. "What if we ordered pizza?"

At the mention of his favorite word, Tad began bouncing in my lap and clapping his hands together. I could see a twinkle of interest in Thomas' eyes, so I nodded.

"Alright," I told them. "Pizza it is."

"With extra anchovies!" Thomas cheered.

Standing, I ruffled his hair and I took them both by the hand. We walked to the closest nurse's station to use the phone. After ordering, and relaying specific instructions for a pizza with extra anchovies though I knew Thomas would never eat it, we went to the small conference room across from their mother's hospital room. I'd reserved the room for the duration to give the family room to spread out. On the table and on the floor there were toys, electronics and anything else my family would need to get through this time. The color of the rooms wasn't as sterile as the rest of the hospital as it was a dull pink with old flowering prints on the wall. My mother was already there, waiting. Seeing the boys she opened her arms and smiled. They ran right into her arms and she hugged them close.

The jealousy over the ease and love of their relationship nearly choked me. I did my best to shake it off and sat down.

"Where's your dad?" My mother asked them.

"He's taking a break," Thomas said, nodding his head in a serious fashion.

"Ah," she said. "Good idea. I bet he needed it. What do you say we get you some dinner?"

"Auntie Tabby already ordered us pizza!" Tad said excitedly.

When my mother's eyes crossed to me, the warmth drained from them and left a marked chill in the room.

"Pizza huh?" She asked. Then looking at the boys she smiled again. "Well I suppose that will have to do."

My mother played with the boys for a time, leaving me to my own devices. After a while Jonathan joined us, followed by the promised pizza. When Thomas saw the large pizza with extra anchovies he cracked a smile. Though no one ate it, it had been worth making him smile, if just for a moment. The three other pizzas had been more than enough.

"Thank you Tabitha," Jon had come up behind me as I watched the boys dig in.

I nodded. I would do anything for my family. He put his hand on my shoulder and I put my hand over his to anchor that feeling of support. I know he didn't blame me. He leaned in close and I could feel his breath on my neck.

"I'm going to be pulling the plug in the next hour," he said. "You should go say goodbye, then I want you to go home. There's nothing more you can do. Your father will be here soon to take care of your mother. I feel like she might turn on you and cause a scene if you're here when it happens."

I nodded again, swallowing past the lump that had formed in my throat. I know it's not that he didn't want me there, it's that she was the boy's grandmother. He needed to keep a good relationship with her and kicking me out was the lesser of two evils. I recognized the logic of his decision and accepted it. Even though it hurt. I stood.

"Alright boys," I smiled at them. "I have to go."

The chorus of disappointment almost made me feel better, as did the hugs I received from them. I turned and Jonathan squeezed my arm as I walked out the door, closing the door behind me. I stared at the numbers 312 as if it were a poisonous snake. Breathing through my teeth, I walked over and through the door before I lost my courage again.

As the door slowly clicked closed behind me I struggled to breathe. My sister's chest rose and fell in time with the beeping and whooshing of the machines that kept her anchored to life. Soon those machines would be turned off and she would no longer be anchored. She would float away like a boat untethered. I heard wracking sobs, so I looked around for a source. The burning in my chest was distracting me, and realized that the wrenching noise was coming from me. I couldn't breathe. I stumbled forward to the bed and sat next to Samantha. My sister. Sam. It was hard to say her name, let alone think it. My entire torso seemed to collapse in on itself. There was a sucking vortex in my chest where my heart used to be. My sister, my best friend, was going to die today, in one hour. How do I cope with that?

Eventually my sobs grew slower and my breathing finally became even. How do you say it? How do you say goodbye to the only good thing in your life? Exhaustion finally began taking over and I knew it was time to leave. Touching her hand, I began to step away when her hand jerked.

"Sam?" Hope sharp and sweet burst through me. I touched her hand again, but there was nothing. The hope that had been born died just as swift and with it returned the crushing loneliness. I turned to leave again but was held back by a hand on my wrist, strong and tight. Looking back, my sister's hand was gripping my wrist so tightly that her fingers bent at odd angles. Her eyes sat open, vacant and her mouth moved like a fish out of water. The machines began to trill noisily. Finally, like an old transistor radio, sound began to pour from her mouth. My sister looked through me, rather than at me. The hand on my wrist hurt but I was too stunned to pull away. At first the sound fountaining from her was jumbled words, then as if the radio had found the right dial, it became a message.

"Challenge Talent Gradual Handy Haversham Candles Candles Fire Water Air Earth, find them Find the Elements. Find your Element. You must find them before you are taken. You will be taken. Take heed child! Run."

A knock on the door broke whatever it was and my sister's hand became limp. She seemed to shrivel in on herself, mummifying before my eyes. The grotesquery of the situation was worsened as the machines continued to breathe for her. The heartbeat that was left barely registered on the machine. My sister was dead. Of this I was sure.

The doctor entered the room soon after the knock and smiled politely at me. He didn't seem surprised by my sister's state so I made a quick exit. Before I could run, as the specter had suggested, my mother grabbed the same wrist that had been crushed just moments ago. As I attempted to push by, I cried out in pain.

"Oh hush," she said. "I barely touched you. You should be ashamed of yourself."

"Mother I don't have time for this," I cried as I tried to leave.

"You should be ashamed," She dug a finger into my chest. "Trying to steal your own sister's husband before she's cold. How dare you?"

"What are you talking about?"

"I saw you two, whispering in the corner, the way he touched you" she spat. "And in front of the children. Have you no shame?"

"Whatever mom," I pushed past her and continued down the hall, my throbbing wrist a reminder of the message.

"You're dead to me!" She said. "You hear me? Dead!"

It was not a surprise to hear, as I was reserving my attention for what was happening to me it was hard to react. I waved behind me and left the hospital as quickly as possible. I needed to take a breath and gauge my mental state. So, for the first time in days, I went home.

 My tiny brownstone seemed like the perfect utopia at the moment. I closed the door behind me and leaned heavily against it. I'd convinced myself that I'd imagined everything on the long walk home. Avoiding taking a cab, I'd used the busy streets of New York to comfort me. The hive of activity on the streets always reminded me of the constant running thoughts in my own mind. It was a rare moment when my thoughts, just like the city, were not racing along.

During my walk I'd felt the hair on the back of my neck stand on end and I looked for a reason, but I had come up empty so I'd continued on. I was probably just feeding into my paranoia over the events from the last day. The safety and security of my little home surrounded me and I breathed in the scent of lemon and lilac. My two favorite smells.

Pushing away from the door I moved to the security panel next to the door, setting the alarm and locking the doors. I may love this city but I wasn't stupid. Walking to my kitchen I started a pot of coffee, out of habit more than need, and scrounged through the fridge for dinner. Though I'd eaten some of the pizza I'd bought for the boys, I was ravenous from the walk.

A glance at the clock over the oven told me it was just shy of ten o'clock at night. A pang squeezed my heart at the realization that Sam was gone. My eyes were dry, but not from a lack of wanting to cry. They burned and as I rubbed them I realized they were filled with grit. I sighed and turned off the coffee pot. It was probably inadvisable to strain my already exhausted eyes.

Mentally and physically exhausted, I climbed the stairs to my loft bedroom. All thoughts of food were forgotten as I struggled to hold my eyes open. Fully dressed I dropped to my mattress and thought dully about kicking my shoes off. Before I could work up the energy to follow through with this line of thoughts I dropped into oblivion.

The dryness of my throat and the gurgling of my stomach is what woke me. Running my tongue across the sandiness of my teeth told me I should probably give them a brush as well. Blinking the sleep from my eyes, I looked blearily for my alarm clock. Seeing that it was three o'clock in the morning I stretched and sat up. Frowning I realized I never took my shoes off, so I corrected that oversight. As I took them off, I looked around my room and sighed. It was a mess. Piles of clothes covered the floor. The only clean spot in the whole room was my bed.

All around me I studied my inexpensive, oft found at flea markets, furniture. The only place I didn't scrimp was my bed. Sleep, to me, was the most important part of my day. It sounds odd, stated as such, but I can't function properly without a good night's rest. It was a tall king size bed with a firm mattress, covered in a pillow top to give it that firm yet soft back support. I stood and pulled the blankets straight. I'd never even made it under the covers. After patting the pillows, I walked to the bathroom to brush my teeth. I stared at the woman moving the brush back and forth inside her mouth and had a hard time finding myself. This woman had hair mussed not just from a night's sleep, but from days of neglect. Dark bruises shadowed under her eyes, belying her lack of sleep. Completely make-upless, she stared hard eyed and blinked away the glimmer of moisture that threatened to spill out.

Turning away from the mirror, I moved through my room to the stairs and down, where I planned to rewarm that pot of coffee I had abandoned the night before. Lack of sleep could explain my delusions from the day before. I shook my head, baffled by the disappearance of my trusted logic in favor of the belief in fantasy. As I reached the bottom of the stairs, I noticed right away that the alarm wasn't set.

Frowning, I looked into the kitchen and back to the alarm. Shrugging I reset the alarm, watched it blink green in confirmation, then moved into the kitchen. I had been so tired when I got home yesterday I must not have set it when I thought I did. As I grabbed the pot to refill the water it sloshed and hot coffee hit my wrist. Hissing, I set the pot back on the burner and ran cold water over the injury.

"Ouch," I muttered. Had I been sleepwalking when I came home? I know I tried to start the coffee but I was sure that I had turned it off before going upstairs. As I was soaking my hand, light filtering through the window over the sink caught my eye.

"That can't be," I said confused. Using my good hand, I bent the blinds to see that I was right. It was day time. So it wasn't three in the morning, it was three in the afternoon. Had I really slept for over eighteen hours? I saw my tiny little back yard that I shared with the brownstone behind mine. The neighbor's twelve-year-old played with the new puppy his parents had finally gotten him for his birthday this year. I smiled at the familiarity of the scene and let the blinds go, concentrating on my hand again.

I turned off the tap and heard an echoing water shut off in the half bath off my kitchen. Immediately on edge, I reached for a kitchen knife. Before I could even pull it completely out of the block the bathroom door opened and out walked my sister. She smiled brightly while she dried her hands. The knife fell from my hands and clattered noisily to the floor.

"Well good morning sunshine," she laughed her familiar laugh and lobbed the balled up paper towel into the trash can. When she made it she whooped. "Two points!"

"But..." I stammered.

"I thought for sure you'd sleep all day," she said turning to the fridge. "Hot date last night?"

"I..." My brain was having a very difficult time forming words. "How?"

"How'd I get in?" She looked at me oddly. "You gave me a key when you moved in and the alarm code is my birthday so... yeah. You ok? You look kinda green."

"I need to sit down," I weaved drunkenly to the kitchen island and sat stiffly.

"Hey, are you ok, really?" She asked. "You look sick. Stupid, of course you are. No wonder you slept so late. You never sleep in."

Sam thumped her head like she was trying to knock sense into it. An old habit so familiar my eyes began leaking before I even realized I was crying.

"Oh, hey, it's ok," she said. "Do you want me to come back? I know I'm imposing, asking you to help me plan my five year anniversary."

"No!" I scrambled up and crushed her against me. "No."

"Alright, no worries sis," she tried to pull away but I resisted so she hugged me back. "Sounds like you had a hell of a night. Wanna talk about it?"

"No," I said as I pulled away and looked at her. "Just a bad dream. What did you say we were planning?"

"Duh, my five year anniversary to Jonathan," she said. Reopening up the fridge, she pulled out the exact same cheese and meat plate we'd snacked on during the planning process several days ago.

I listened to her talk about the plans she was never going to actually act on because it had all been a diversion. While we were planning her fake anniversary party, Jonathan was calling all of the people in my address book she had slipped to him earlier. I laughed softly at the thought. I didn't care that I'd really fallen off the deep end. It wasn't realistic to think that I was reliving the past or that my dream had been an extremely vivid, an accurate vision of the future. So I accepted the fact that my sister, as real as she seemed right at the moment, couldn't in fact be real.

I must just be having a hallucination. Though I knew and accepted that, I still enjoyed the fact that she was here in front of me. Living, breathing, and solidly real, at least for me. I watched her flip her hair effortlessly in a way I had always envied. A cold shudder ran through me with the motion as I watched her move. Something seemed off and I couldn't quite put my finger on it. So I observed her while she chattered about the surprise party. Then I saw it. Because it was something I had always envied, I knew every step of the flip and noticed that she was using the wrong hand in execution. I had tried to replicate her small hair twist and flip for years, but I'd never been able to do it just right or achieve the natural fluidness of the move. This person had matched the effortlessness. However, Samantha had been right hand dominant, the person before me was left handed. It was as if I were looking into a mirror and watching my sister. Everything was backward.

Smiling, I nodded at what she was saying and moved to the coffee pot. This wasn't my sister and it definitely wasn't a hallucination. I poured a cup of coffee to cover the shaking of my hands and give myself a moment to work through this logically. If this was a hallucination, why would I insert imperfection? I had been perfectly content to accept and live in this fake world a moment ago. So why would I invent something to draw me out? Knowing myself as I did, I was aware that I preferred fabrication to reality, but chose to live in reality. I enjoyed romance and fantasy, but I knew that a life with those things would set me up to fail. I drank the hot coffee slowly, trying to puzzle it out.

My sister laughed to herself about something while I looked at the back of my hand where I'd burned it earlier. It was red and slightly raised, but thankfully not blistered. Because it burned slightly still, I went back to the small window over the sink and picked a piece of my aloe plant that lived there. Absently, I raised the blinds so that the plant was able to soak in the impromptu sunshine. I watched the neighbor boy running around with his puppy, listening to their happy yips and squeals.

Suddenly exhausted again, I yawned and realized I'd never picked up the knife that I'd dropped earlier. As I stooped to pick it up something occurred to me. There was a way to test this hallucination, or whatever it was. If I proved it wasn't real it would go away, but how could I do that? What if she really was my sister? Should I stab her? Cut her somehow? Or if I just run the knife across the back of my hand would the pain should banish this false apparition, if that is indeed what it is.

I frowned and decided to carry out the plan because it seemed the safer course. Even if my sister were a delusion created by my sleep starved brain, I would never be able to hurt her. Taking the knife, I turned toward the person pretending to by my sister, who was frowning at me.

"Tab," she narrowed her eyes. "What are you thinking?"

"I'm working on a new theory," I replied and ran the sharp blade through my upturned palm. I was suddenly very glad my knives were sharpened on a regular basis. It took a moment for the pain to set it, but when it did, it was ferocious.

Instead of disappearing or coming to my aid with a "what the hell", my sister just sat there at the island and stared at me. Her body spasmed as her lips slowly curled upwards in a smile and she licked her lips. A shudder ran through me and I backed up against the kitchen counter.

"Well," my sister's voice had dropped several octaves and was now barely recognizable. "Looks like you're offering something I'm willing to take."

I watched in horror as her lips continued to curl upward and fold back over her face, exposing her teeth-turned-razors shoved in sickly greying gums. Before the monster could even make a move, I turned to the window thinking only of escape. But glass had been replaced by ugly cement blocks, mortared and solid. Trying to make a break for it, I ran for the front door and threw it open, finding only more of the same ugly grey blocks. Looking over my shoulder I noticed the monster on the floor where my blood had dripped, lapping at it like a kitten would lap at a saucer of milk. A shudder ran through my body at the image this thing created. It still partially wore my sister's body and I could see parts of her face, folded backward like some grotesque plastic Halloween mask.

A pounding on the other side of the brick wall caught my attention, as well as the attention of the monster.

"Go away!" It shouted between slurps.

"Help!" I screamed and pounded back.

The pounding paused, then intensified until dust was breaking free. A voice in my head told me I should probably step back, so I backed up a few of the stairs. I could see that the monster was still licking at the floor, where the last drops of my blood lay. Soon the grout from between the bricks began to come loose and I saw a curling vine poke through the cracks. Before I could even process that water began leaking through, slow at first, then faster as the pressure continued to break more grout away. A cement block fell from the doorway and a gush of water came forth, followed by an enormous vine that crushed the blocks in its path. It wasn't long before the entire thing came crashing down with a flood of water. The monster gave a cry as what was left of my blood was washed away. Its eyes, located deep in its gaping throat, locked on me and it gave an odd howling sound as it rushed forward.

Not giving a thought as to what may be on the other side of the doorway I jumped through, where arms caught and steadied me. Before I could get my bearings and thank my savior, a pain exploded behind my eyes and darkness surrounded me.

The sound of muffled voices woke me. I did my best to keep still but I must have twitched because the voices ceased. Listening closely, I could hear the rustling of clothes as people moved around me, but the bag still hung over my face. I could feel that my arms were bound behind me to a metal chair. A small feeling of relief trickled in as I realized my legs were unbound. A whisper and then a hushing from nearby had me jerking toward the sudden sound. If my captors saw the movement there was no reaction. A headache throbbed dully at the base of my neck and radiated through my skull. Groaning slightly I attempted to stretch my shoulders, which proved incredibly difficult as I was bound.

"Ok," I said grumpily into the silence. "I know you're there, so why doesn't someone tell me what's happening. I assume this is just my delusional breakdown, so can we please continue onward and I can get comfortable."

"Why aren't you scared?" Someone, a woman asked.

"Because this isn't real," I replied flippantly.

"She isn't ready," a man with a deep voice stated.

"She has to be," another man replied. "She doesn't have a choice."

"Well then," the first woman sighed. "Neither do we."

At that the cover was removed from my head and the light seared my retinas. I closed my eyes until my hands were unbound, then I whipped my hands in front of my face to shield my eyes from the rude amount of brightness in the room. That's when I realized that it wasn't a fluorescent light that gave off the bright, warm glow. I blinked my eyes to help them adjust to the intensity of hundreds of tiny yellow suns dancing around the small room. Larger than fireflies, I couldn't consider them any sort of insect.

Immediately I wanted to study them, but when I reached out to hold one in my palm it singed my hand. I gasped and pulled my hand back. A tiny, perfectly round, red welt sat at the apex my palm.

A chuckle echoed around me and had the entirety of the tiny globes moving upward just overhead. They had been obscuring my view of the room at large I realized and my three captors stood several feet away. Two men and a woman, the voices I had heard only moments ago.

One man towered toward the ceiling, where the globes busily got out of the way of his movements. A grin split his wide face, the color of good rich mocha, with eyes to match and a shiny bald head. He seemed to be excited by the entire prospect of my kidnapping, barely containing a chuckle, which he did his best to cover with his hand and a cough. With his other hand he held a tiny woman close, who was also beaming at me. She was stunning. Tiny and perfect, she came up to the man's chest, roughly a few inches shorter than my average height. With a blonde pixie cut and bright blue eyes she was everything I wasn't with my dark lanky hair and bookish looks. I could only imagine what I looked like. Over the last twenty-four hours I'd slept fully clothed and probably hadn't showered in days.

As my eyes fell upon the final person in the room I thought dully about being thankful I'd brushed my teeth before going downstairs. Though the other two were beautiful and obviously deeply caring for one another, the man who I studied now seemed their opposite. He glowered at me as if he despised my very existence. While his dark hair matched my coloring, it hung shabbily. He'd cared for it at some point in the last couple days, but perhaps had experienced an altercation with a lawn mower recently. It shot off in crazy spikes as if he had dragged his hands through it often, curling lightly is random disarray.

As if sensing my thoughts, he ran his hand through it and grimaced. Stubble covered his chin and dark circles ran under his bright green eyes. His disheveled appearance almost made me feel better about my seemingly homeless attire. The intensity of his stare and scorching dislike had me breaking eyes contact and coughing. I looked down at my feet and noted that I didn't even have shoes on. I wiggled my toes lightly as I noticed some of my toes poked out of holes in my socks.

"Well," I sighed. "If this really is my delusion, how do I get a shower and some new clothes?"

"Still think this isn't real?" The disheveled man demanded. "You've been attacked several times in the last couple days, felt actual pain and outsmarted a doppelganger. How is this a delusion?"

"There have been plenty of studies of complete mental breaks where the patient completely immerses themselves in an alternate reality because they cannot live their lives for whatever reason," looking back at him I was confused by his anger. "I thought perhaps pain would waken me from this decidedly nightmarish delusion, but since it has not then I must be more immersed than is usual, but which is also documented. Being stuck in your own mind is a rarity but not improbable. Especially when compared with the reality which you present to be real."

I chuckled to myself at the thought. Though he seemed annoyed still, I caught a glimmer of respect in his eyes.

"I apologize," I cleared my throat, the sound gravelly from disuse. "I do not speak often. The gravity and tenor of my speech pattern has been termed off-putting in the past. However, I think I shall make an exception in this instance since it is my fantasy and I will be hard pressed to offend figments of my imagination."

Laughing fully, the giant mocha beauty stepped forward and pulled me into a hug. Not realizing how much I needed the connection, I teared up slightly, and hugged him back.

"Thank you," I told him sincerely, wiping the impromptu moisture from my eyes. "I didn't realize how much I needed a hug."

"Not a problem child," his deep voice boomed around the room and the tiny globes danced in excitement at the sound.

"Don't mind Chauncy," the woman stepped forward and offered her hand. "I'm Valerie."

I was inordinately happy to see that my height assessment was accurate. She was just a few inches shorter than myself. It felt shallow, but I was excited to be taller than her. Anyone who was that gorgeous needed to be shorter than average. I took her hand and smiled.

"Hello," I said. "I would introduce myself, but I have the distinct feeling that you all know me."

"That would be true," the disheveled man stepped forward next, but did not extend a hand. "I'm Alexandar."

Something told me it was a good thing we didn't touch yet. Electricity seemed to crackle between us.

"Yes," I agreed approvingly. "You are."

I realized too late that I had spoken aloud and my embarrassment was clear on my face.

"Did you know that most mammals have a gland at the top of their nose, called the vomeronasal organ? It's believed this detects the pheromones related to sex and triggers an involuntary response," I smiled awkwardly while internally I cringed.

Great save Tab, I thought.

Alexandar's frown deepened, Chauncy chortled in delight and Valerie stepped forward taking my hand.

"I think we are going to be great friends," she told me. "Can you feel it?"

"Yes," I replied honestly. "Though I'm not sure I should trust my feelings as you all did just kidnap me."

"Kidnap you?!" Alexandar exploded.

Attempting to take a step back from the anger, I tripped and fell back into the chair. Thankfully, Valerie was still holding my hand and gentled my fall. I looked up at her gratefully. Though this seemed to be my delusion, it has not helped my grace.

"Now Alex," Chauncy cautioned. "What else is she going to think after the last couple days?"

"I don't know," Alexandar muttered under his breath, then louder. "But at the least she could be grateful that we SAVED her."

"She seemed to be working through things well enough," Valerie defended me. "It wouldn't have been long before she figured out how to kill the beast. I have faith in her."

"Thank you," I nodded. "I think."

"You're welcome," Valerie smiled airily at me. "Let's get you cleaned up."

"Yes please," I sighed in relief.

"Yeah, you look like a disaster," Alexandar retorted.

"You don't look so comely yourself, sir," I replied. "You may consider a hot shower of your own."

Chauncy seemed to break into uncontrollable laughter as Valerie swept me out of the room. A last look over my shoulder had Alex turning and punching the giant, only to be descended upon by the globes as if they were a hive of bees protecting their queen.

"Well," Valerie said as we walked down a dark hallway lit by torches. "That was quite an impression you made. Let's make him eat those words."

"I believe that would be remarkably pleasant, Valerie," I slipped my arm around hers and continued down the hall.

"Please, call me Val," she told me.

"And you can call me Tabbie," I patted her arm with my other hand. "It's odd, I feel more at home with you in this delusion than I ever have in my real life. I think I like it here and I feel it may be remiss to return, though reality may eventually come crashing back."

"Sooner than you think," Valerie agreed.

Bathing in a hot spring was something I'd always wanted to do. To feel the naturally hot water flow over my naked body and float as if no one and nothing mattered. Who knew I'd just have to go crazy first.

I giggled aloud and listened to it reverberate off the cave walls. The hot springs smelled of sulfur and something I couldn't quite put my finger on, and it felt absolutely wonderful. I'd dreamed of one day traveling to Japan with my sister and experiencing an authentic Onsen. Perhaps one high up in the mountains, surrounded by snow.

At the moment however, this hot spring was just what I had needed to clean myself and feel rejuvenated. The small underground cave was filled with the soft flickering light of torches and the rushing sound of a river that echoed down a different corridor than I'd come in through. It was a soothing experience that would be hard to recreate in my bathtub with some white noise.

Before today, I never would have floated naked in the pool. I would have modestly asked for a bathing suit, out of fear that someone would walk in and see my nakedness. I don't even like to look at myself in the mirror after taking a shower. Avoiding looking at my reflection I would towel off, dress, and then assess the result. I wouldn't consider myself a prude, not in the slightest. I understood the mechanics of sexual encounters, but due to my crippling awkwardness had not had the opportunity to experience them first hand. I believed in sex before marriage, especially if you wanted to truly test your eternal compatibility. Statistically, more than fifty percent of marriages fail. In my opinion if couples believed in testing their relationship as rigorously as their new cars, they might know whether they were meant to be together.

But what did I know? I'm just a virgin, who has never had anyone care about me enough to attempt bridging my awkwardness. I've found that most men find my awkwardness an oddity, when I finally open up enough to try talking I usually find myself staring at their retreating backs. I wish I could blame my unquenchable thirst for knowledge, but I enjoy learning new things too much to place blame there.

Hearing a noise, I dipped my body down so that I was treading water. A shiver ran through my body, regardless of the heat that surrounded me, as I made eye contact with Alexandar.

"How long were you staring at me?" I asked, curious rather than accusing.

"I..." His face flamed a deep red and I surmised that a long time was probable.

Rather than feeling shame at the thought of someone staring at my naked body while I was deep in thought, I felt an odd sensation. Almost like a rising bubble in my stomach, glowing and radiating a deep sense of satisfaction. I smiled with the feeling and watched his face grow even deeper. I saw that he was holding a towel and a new set of clothing.

"Are those for me?" I asked moving to the side of the pool to hold the rock and steady my fast beating heart.

"Umm..." He shook himself visibly. "Yes."

Clearing his throat Alexandar slid to the side, setting the pile of cloth on a nearby rock. His eyes never left mine. A heat kindled in my stomach that I recognized as desire, though I'd never felt it before. I'd read many books on the subject, especially while researching other cultures and their societal beliefs on intercourse while working on my dissertation: The Art of Sex. My subject had been approved so quickly my head spun. And oddly I had a lot of interest from subjects willing to help, including tenured professors, until they understood the premise of my work. Which was just to point out that sex has been selling since the dawn of time. Watching Alexandar watch me was unsettling. He looked...hungry. The disheveled boy from before seemed to have disappeared and if I'd thought his green eyes were bright before, they seemed to glow in the low light of the torches, reminding me of a cat. His face still had the stubble and dark circles under the intensity of his eyes, but he seemed frozen in place. I grinned at him. I had a theory and there was only one way to test it. Perhaps my problem previous to this experience had been talking, though he didn't seem to be scared of my intelligence earlier. Besides, it was high time I took control of my fantasies.

"Were you planning on joining me?" I asked.

As I asked, I watched the hunger deepen in his gaze, then just as quickly it was gone and replaced with derision. I wondered if I'd imagined it completely.

"That's the type of woman you are?" Alexandar spit. "You'd jump into bed with the first stranger to see you naked after the last couple days?"

"I suppose so," I laughed at his incredulity and refused to be hurt by his easy dismissal of my invitation. "If you're not interested you are welcome to leave so my nakedness does not offend your tender sensibilities."

I moved away from the wall and toward the little ladder off to the side. As I began to climb, I heard a rustle of fabric and retreating footsteps. Though the sound gave me pleasure to have won the small skirmish, I felt slightly disappointed that he hadn't stayed to battle wills with me. Something told me we would be well matched. I looked forward to the next time and wondered idly why he was holding back. I reached the pile and took the towel carefully from beneath the small pile of clothes to dry off.

Once I was dried and dressed, I padded barefoot and comfortable in the loose fitting clothing toward the tunnel that had brought me to the hot springs. When I found the long corridor that held many of the other tunnels and doorways, I wondered where I was supposed to go next. I hadn't been given any instructions and my stomach was rumbling noisily. I heard music and laughter, so I followed the sound hoping to find food.

On the left and several doors down I found an archway that led into an enormous dining room. The abundance of food was staggering. Mountainous heaps on silver serving dishes. Silver goblets and crystal wine glasses were lined next to a shining punch bowl, looking incredibly inviting. Following my stomach, I grabbed a plate that had already been prepared and nibbled at pieces of turkey, rolls, fruit and candied yams. I grabbed a glass and filled it with the punch and sipped. The honeyed wine coated my tongue and easily slipped down my throat, warming my stomach.

I turned toward the laughter and conversation. Taking the only seat available I sat down in the empty chair across from Valerie, who smiled widely then turned back to Chauncy. Though they were nearly ten feet from each other, they seemed to be having an intimate conversation. She and I sat across at the center and the men sat on either end of the table. This table was expansive, easily twenty feet long. I glanced at Alexandar who was just glaring at his plate, picking at his food. Ignoring him I ate in silence, absorbing the light and laughter coming from the other end of the table.

A longing began to creep up as I watched Valerie and Chauncy. Their obvious love for each other was so bright and alive it was intoxicating. Though that also could have been the wine. I wasn't a habitual imbiber, though there was an occasional function where I had a drink or two.

Looking at the cup I saw that I had chosen a silver goblet. Inscribed was a picture of a sailor's compass. The eight pointed star gleamed in the torchlight. As I stared, the star wavered and began to turn. It wobbled and spun like an actual compass. Abruptly it stopped, pointing true North and the seat to my right. Frowning, I looked up and into the intensity of his gaze. Had I thought they glowed before? Now they seemed to burn. He pushed up from the table and my heart stuttered as he walked toward me, then past and out of the room.

As my lungs burned, I gulped in air and I realized I'd been holding my breath again. Looking down I saw that the goblet had righted itself, with North pointing upward and etched unmoving into the chalice. Frowning, I looked up into Valerie's smiling eyes.

"What," I asked. "Was that?"

"That was just nature taking its course," Valerie replied. Let out a belching laugh that shook the entire table.

"I don't understand what that means." I stated to the room at large.

Seeming to have lost my appetite, I pushed up from the table and crossed to a fireplace. It was large enough that I could have stepped into it fully extended, if there had not been a fire within. I was cold after this interaction and sought the warmth the fire promised. Valerie followed me and rubbed my arms.

"I felt the same when I was chosen," she said. "Lost, confused, and overwhelmed."

"That's just it," I told her while I watched the flames dance. "I'm none of those things. I've accepted that I've had some mental breakdown and this will be my new life."

I looked down and studied the fully healed scar that ran down my arm, which just hours before had been running deep and bloody.

"This looks like the wound happened months ago, rather than hours," I said. "And I have no explanation for that. I'm confused, but I'm not overwhelmed. I'm confused for different reasons than I should be. I've accepted that this may be my new reality and that what happens to me hurts, but I also realize that I can control and influence what happens in this reality. So my confusion stems from the fact that I'm happy here. I've created a reality where I feel accepted and loved immediately upon entering it, which is my true fantasy. There's also guilt, because I left my nephews without a mother and an aunt."

"We've made some calls," Chauncy replied.

"I suppose I should thank you," I responded. "But my guilt stems from the fact that I don't want to go back, not really."

"You've had a tragedy in your life," Valerie stated. "Of course you don't want to be immersed in your grief."

"I appreciate your thoughts," I said. "Both of you. I do have a question though."

"What's that?" Valerie asked.

"How my wound healed?" I flexed my hand.

"Are you sure you're ready for the truth?" Chauncy asked walking closer. Sitting in one of the four wide leather chairs near the fire, he pulled Valerie into his lap.

"I can't see why I wouldn't be," I said. "I still don't believe this is all real so I suppose I could attempt to come up with my own answer, but at the moment I'm interested in what my subconscious has to say. Please continue."

"You're a trip," Chauncy chuckled, shaking his head.

"Thank you," I said. "This is the most I've spoken outside of lecture halls than I can remember. My lack in understanding of social nuances can cripple any conversation."

"Well we are happy to help ease that," Valerie said.

"As to your wound, the answer is simple," Chauncy redirected. "It's magic."

"Hmm," I nodded. "Since this is my fantasy, I can see how my subconscious would insert magic. In a twisted way, it's logical. Continue."

"The four of us," he said. "We are the Council of Elements."

"Elements?" I queried. "As in Earth, Air and such?"

"Exactly," Valerie said. "Yes."

"Our group has existed since the beginning of time," Chauncy continued. "If you'd like we can take you to the library, where you can read about the traditions."

"You said the four of us," I stated. "You include me in this count?"

"Yes," Chauncy answered.

"Why me?" I wondered. "I doubt I was voted in."

"It doesn't work like that," Valerie stated. "This Council is formed by the elements. You are chosen at a point where the world thinks you are ready to assume your duties."

"Duties?" I asked.

"That I will leave you to read about," Chauncy rose and set Valerie on her feet. "For some it is easier to see what we can do and others would rather read about it in books than accept it from someone they don't completely trust yet. I'm guessing you are the latter."

"Hmm," I pondered this and nodded. What could it hurt really to read? I enjoyed reading and perhaps I would find a clue to my own diagnosis in these books, even if it was one delivered by my own subconscious.

Chauncy held his hand out to me and I put mine in his large palm, marveling at the difference in size. My hand was eclipsed in his and yet he was gentle when folding it within. I smiled up at him and followed his urging toward the door and down the hallway to an ornately carved wooden door. It shone like it was lovingly made and well taken care of. The unicorns, nymphs, dryads and faeries seemed to move within their natural canvas as I walked underneath its arches.

I was so enchanted by the carving that I was simply stunned when I looked away and into the enormity of what was the largest library I had ever seen. It stretched so far in all directions that I was unable to tell where it ended, or if it even did. My surprise and pleasure was apparent when what could only be described as a squeal of delight escaped me. I wanted to run giggling through the racks and find out if the library did end, because I secretly hoped that it didn't.

Barely able to restrain myself long enough to look at my companion, who seemed to be getting pleasure from the simple joy I was exuding. He led me farther in and after walking a while, turned and led me to a nice sitting area. A small fire crackled in the hearth, making the area seem homier than a library had a right to be. I sighed at a sudden pang of homesickness.

Shaking off the feeling I sighed. When it was time I would return to the reality I left behind, better off for the little mental vacation. With a smile slightly more forced than I would have liked, I turned and looked up at Chauncy. He seemed to sense my internal struggle and squeezed my hand before letting it fall.

"This is my favorite area," he told me. "This is where I learned to read."

"How long have you been here?" I asked, curious enough to know how my subconscious would answer.

"I was chosen when I was a teenager," Chauncy stated. He turned back toward a wall near the fire. On it there was an enormous filing system with small index card sized drawers.

It was so large that he had to pull a metal chain to roll the entire system for a long time. While he searched through the many drawers he told me his story.

"I was raised on the street," he said with his back to me. "Quite literally."

Intermittently he would stop the revolution and take out an index card, setting it aside.

"I lived out of cars when I was lucky, cardboard boxes and bridges when I wasn't. My mother, loosely termed, was an addict and a prostitute. She scored drugs for herself rather than feeding me or finding us shelter. I found myself caring for her more often than she cared for me. I did so under the mistaken belief that she would get better. There were very few bright spots that would fuel my hope. They fueled them perhaps even more urgently because they were so few. Those were the days that she would look at me and recognize me as her son. She would cry and hold me and apologize for the pain she was putting me through. Each time I believed her when she swore she would get help and we could be happy, really happy."

He paused and seemed to study an index card for an extended period of time before setting it aside and beginning again.

"A day came when I was thirteen, while in the middle of one of these rock bottom promises, she suggested that I follow her into her line of work. She suggested that she could get better more easily if we had some extra money to help out. We'd be able to stay in a house, maybe get a dog. I found myself believing her, until she mentioned that she already had clients lined up for me."

Chancy stopped working just for a moment then continued with a sigh as if this was a story he were tired of telling.

"She had men ready to pay me for certain services. Services that I had listened to for as long as I could remember. Things that could put her in the hospital if the John was a little too overeager. At that moment I knew I had a decision to make. I could stay and live the life that would get me killed or I could leave. Have you ever seen a fork in the road and known it for what it was?"

Chauncy looked over his shoulder and I nodded. I knew that feeling well. Looking at a decision and realizing, whichever way you chose, it would affect the life you've chosen for yourself.

Chauncy turned back to the rolling rack.

"I had no hope that it would get better as she promised. I could leave her and find another life. It was terrifying, the thought that I would leave everything I'd ever known. So I chose. I made a decision that I have not once regretted. I chose the harder road, but because of this the elements chose me."

He turned to me with a small stack of index cards and handed them over.

"Does it get easier when you tell the story?" I asked.

Chauncy shook his head and chuckled.

"I enjoy that your question is in regards to storytelling and not my welfare," he said.

"That's not..." My face flamed at the thought that he would think that I was diminishing his experiences.

"No, you misunderstand," he said. "It was your complete lack of judgement, your focus on the technicalities. Your acceptance of my life that I lived. You had no questions about how I was able to overcome, no questions about how I could leave my mother like that. Just a question about the retelling of a difficult story. It's refreshing."

I frowned and wondered what my subconscious was attempting to imply.

"I will leave you now. I have a feeling you would like to locate the volumes on your own, so I will leave you to your solitude."

"Wait," I stopped him before he could turn and leave. "I'm confused."

"Why?"

"I don't know what your story is trying to reveal to me about my diagnosis," I said plainly.

"Well," Chancy chuckled. "Maybe you should wonder if it's your subconscious at all."

I continued to frown at his retreating back and tried to puzzle out what had just happened. It was indeed confusing. While I had never experienced abuse in the truest sense of the word, there had always been a chasm between my mother and I. It had been unbreachable for as long as I could remember and I could never understand why. Perhaps Chauncy's story was just bringing my own horrid story into perspective. That my life could have been worse. I could have had no support at all. I was lucky to have had a sister that loved and care for me. Nodding, I looked at the first index card and smiled at the familiar Dewey Decimal System of numbers that was scrolled across the top. The title of the book was simple: The Origin of the Elemental Council.

I put the rest of the index cards in my back pocket and began to search the stacks. As I moved I let my free hand reach out and caress the volumes. The musk of well used leather and parchment surrounded me all my life. Before I could read I would sit down with a book and turn the pages, just to catch the scent of knowledge. I would stare at the letters on the pages and make up my own stories before I truly dove into a book. Looking back at the index card I looked for the last name of the author: Catacomb.

At the end of a row of stacks I looked up to find the letters. The rows in front of me were the normal size of library stacks, but farther in I saw stacks that reached upward higher than I could see. It was dizzying.

Shaking my head at the enormity of the library, I found the letters that I was looking for. Currently I was in the Gs'. An arrow pointed me left to find the beginning of the alphabet. Following the arrow, I made my way toward the section on the index card. I had been to massive libraries before. Yale, Harvard, Oxford all had several large libraries on their campuses, but this was different. Not knowing exactly how large it was gave the stacks a sense of wonder and enchantment. I always felt that way when surrounded by books; however, this was so much more intense than I had ever experienced. I felt as if I could spend the rest of my life reading and never be unhappy again. This was my version of heaven.

I reached a wall and followed the directions. I had been walking for quite a while and wondered briefly how I would find my way out. Soon I began hearing music and veered off course to find it. Tucking the index card safely with the others, I wandered toward the sound. Wistful, yearning notes hung in the air, a melody that spoke of passion barely restrained. The music seemed to be coming from behind a section of books. I frowned as I reached an area of the stacks where the music seemed loudest. I looked for a doorway but found none. The music continued as I searched the books. My frown deepened and I looked upward. Seeing that I was in the section from the first index card I pulled it back out and realized I was precisely where I needed to be.

The book indicated was sitting exactly where the card said it would be. *The Origin of the Elemental Council* by Catherine Catacombs. I pulled at the book but it was stuck. With both hands I yanked and it pulled straight out then and stopped. A metal clanging and clunking began, like I'd set off a mechanism behind the wall. Slowly the section of wall began to swing outward just far enough that, if I were so inclined, I could slip behind the wall. I stared at it for a time, considering. As the metal clunking sound began I assumed I was out of time and slipped into the unknown for the second time in twenty-four hours.

As the door closed behind me and I quickly realized my mistake. I was left in total darkness. I had not even had time to consider bringing a flashlight and there were no torches lit. As I stood in the darkness my heart began to thud and my breathing became quick and shallow.

By extending my elbows I could touch the walls on either side of me. If I had been prone to claustrophobia I would have been in the middle of a full blown panic attack. It was hard enough to slow my breathing as it was, and unlike many people I harbored no real fear of the dark or tight closed spaces. As my heartbeat slowed and no danger was readily apparent, the music was able to penetrate my addled brain. Slowly I put both hands on either wall and moved toward the sound. As it got louder my heart picked up again, this time more in response to the music than the darkness I was surrounded in.

The walls were made of a solid brick and mortar. I could feel the rows and valleys as I walked. When I found a divot close to the origin of the music I didn't hesitate and reached my hand inside to release a small latch. Instead of a loud mechanical banging that I'd heard earlier, it seemed to be a manual pressure lock. I pushed lightly against the wall and felt the hidden door give as it opened. I pushed harder and opened the door enough to see through. Coming from the still darkness the brightness blinded me for a moment.

It was a relatively small room compared to others I'd seen so far, but still palatial in comparison to what I was used to. What seemed odd was that even though I could see walls, I would have sworn I was outside. Grass grew where carpet or hardwood should have been. Several blooming trees, at various states of flowering, grew and flourished. Flowering vines grew up and around the walls. A sun the size of a basketball glowed brightly in response to the music. Laying in a tree larger than the rest, on a branch that bowed deeply into the shape of a hammock, was Alexandar. His eyes were closed and he picked the strings of what looked like a lute. The branch sway gracefully to the music, as if it were swinging in the breeze. I watched for a time, enchanted by the melody and wary of breaking whatever peace he seemed to be gaining from this time alone. Though his body seemed relaxed, the weeping melody belied a deep sadness within.

I found myself needing to comfort him. A strong urge pushed me forward and I stepped onto the grass. As soon as I did the music stopped, the image shattered, and I stepped into a room like any other. A soft glow came from a nearby fireplace, a small bookcase sat against one wall. Instruments lined an entire wall, along with a piano and a large wooden drawer system labeled "sheet music". Alexandar lay on a large chaise staring at me. Though glaring may have been more accurate. I felt keenly the loss of the garden he had created and wondered if he felt the same. I realized I must have made a grievous error in breaking his solitude. Then I shook my head. It was preposterous to project my imaginings on anyone else, especially if he was a figment of my imagination. I was beginning to forget that this wasn't real. A dangerous road to follow.

"What are you doing here?" Alexandar's voice broke through my musings so I walked fully into the room.

"I'm sorry to disturb you," I said. "I was in the library and found my way here by following the music. What is this place?"

"It's the music room," he said flatly. Standing, he went to the wall and replaced the lute. Then he moved to leave through the open doorway.

"Where are you going?" I asked.

"Away," he said.

"From me?" I surmised.

"Yes from you," he rounded on me in surprising anger. "You're always there. Everywhere I turn you're there."

Stalking forward he stopped directly in front of me. Though his rage was impressive, I was more curious than afraid.

"I can't seem to escape you," he said.

"I apologize for any discomfort I've added to your life," I said sincerely. "As you may recall, my being here wasn't exactly voluntary."

"That's the thing though," his eyes narrowed. "You know you can leave at any time. So why haven't you?"

"I assumed I was being held here," I said.

"Well you know what assume really means," he scoffed.

"Yes, I do," I answered matter of factly.

Alexandar stood there for a moment, mouth working like a fish attempting to breathe before he burst into a deep rumbling laughter. I watched in awe as his face transformed. It was both charming and disarming to see him lower his guard, if for just a glimpse. As he saw that I was studying him, Alexandar's laughter began to dissipate.

"You're being genuine," he said oddly, as if he wasn't used to honesty.

"What else would I be?" I asked.

"Manipulative," he responded quickly.

"What motive would I have?" I wondered aloud.

"That I haven't figured out yet," he stepped closer and brought his face inches from mine. "But if there is one to find, I will find it."

Though we weren't touching there seemed to be electricity running along my body. It was as if the air between us was trying to pull us together, a literal magnetism that I was unable to resist. Just as I began to lean forward to meet it, he took one large step backward. Then, without a word, he turned and left.

I watched Alexandar's exit with an odd sense of yearning. I had the feeling that he'd wanted to close the distance between us, and I know I had wanted him to. What did that say about my state of mind that I felt so comfortable with the idea of essentially making out with myself? I snorted out a laugh. The sound startled me in the empty room but it felt so pleasant to just let myself laugh.

It had been such a long time since I'd allowed myself to laugh that it was satisfying to feel the release of tension I hadn't known was there. More relaxed than I wanted to admit, even to myself, I walked along the wall of instruments, running my hands absently over them. I stopped at the wind section. The wall was set up in four sections and over each section was an elemental symbol. Earth over the wood percussion section holding drums, toms and rain sticks. Air over the wind instruments: flutes, clarinets, and horns. Fire over the string instruments: guitar, violin and bass. And finally, Water over the brass percussive instruments: bells and cymbals.

I'd always been pulled to the trumpet and some of the heavier brass wind instruments. My mother had forced me to learn the violin instead. She'd said that playing an instrument like a man was trashy. I caressed the shiny brass instrument with a longing I'd never really let myself feel. If I was going to get to the bottom of this mental break I needed to let myself feel and experience everything, otherwise I could potentially be stuck here forever.

Turning, I moved to the fire section and picked up the violin and rosined the bow. Without needing music I just let myself play. I'd trained for years and my near photographic memory led the way in my need to express my frustration. Though it surprised me that it was a song that called storms in a video game I used to play. Oddly it released my confusion and frustration. I played like that for a while until my confusion was gone and running with the theme, I moved to another song from the same series that had my blood pumping faster. It would normally be played on a trumpet so I threw myself into it. It was exciting and different. I hadn't even realized I'd coveted the music of these video games until now. I was able to express my frustration and anger. But in the same notes

I was able to convey my excitement over the new world I was experiencing.

When I was finished, I drooped a little. I was suddenly very tired. From the corner, the piano began to play another familiar song. It was the Song of Healing. Tears burned my eyes as I listened to the music. When the music finally faded I put my violin away and waited for the musician to reveal themselves.

"I love the Hyrulian games," Valerie's voice came from the corner. "No matter what was going on in my life I could go home and fight for what was right and just. And win,"

"They were cathartic for me as well," I agreed, taking a deep breathe. "Thank you."

"Of course," she replied. "Any time you want to play nerdy music, I'm down."

"Glad to hear it," I said. "I was never allowed to play music that wasn't composed by someone over a hundred years ago. While I appreciate the Greats, I wanted to play modern music as well. So I did it in secret."

"Understandably," Valerie smiled. "You play very well though."

"Thank you," I said sincerely. "Your skills on the piano are nothing to dismiss off hand."

"I appreciate that," she told me.

"Why are there elemental symbols over the different sections," I wondered.

"Did you have time to read anything?" She asked me.

"No," I said. "The first book I tried to find led me to this secret passageway behind the stacks."

"Ahh," Valerie nodded with a twinkle in her eyes. "Did Chauncy pick out the books for you?"

"Yes," I told her.

"Well played Chauncy," she said quietly. "Well played."

"What does that mean?" I asked pointedly.

"Nothing," she said with a wave of her hand. "He probably just wanted you to find the catacombs, knowing you would be interested in them."

"Well that's true enough," I said. Pulling out the index cards from my back pocket I studied them.

I realized as I looked at them that they all had one thing in common. They all had the word Catacombs, or at least some nod to secret passages. *Catacomb Diaries, The* by Geraldine Fitzgerald. *World of the Secret Catacombs, The* by Michelle Jaxun. *Secret Life of the Elemental, The* by Hennessey Williams. It went on and one. The only one that didn't fit was *Elementals and Their Servants* by Aimee Ratte.

"What did you find?" Valerie asked.

"I found that all of these except one book have some reference to secrets or passageways," I looked up, frowning.

Valerie seemed to be attempting to hide a smile.

"Why is that funny?" I asked.

"No reason," she said and began walking to the door. "Perhaps you should find that last book."

"Hmm," I nodded absently, the weariness I'd felt earlier after purging my emotions had ebbed slightly. I had decided to find the book and curl up somewhere before sleeping with my remaining energy.

"Wait," I called before she could leave. "I have a question."

Valerie turned and nodded for me to continue.

"Why are you here?" I asked. "If the theme I am picking up around why the universe picks us then you had to choose didn't you? Between life and death."

"Yes," her face sobered at the reminder. "It's not a pretty story."

"I would like to hear it, if that's ok," I persisted.

There had to be something in these characters back stories to give me a clue to my escape, no matter how small.

"If you're sure," Valerie stepped back into the room and sat in the chair near the fire, staring into the flames. Then she patted the chair across from her. I followed her direction and sat.

"I know you are struggling with your acceptance of your new world," she said. "So that is why I'm going to tell you my story. It may bring you some perspective to yours. It's an old wound and I'm not fond of exposing it. Are you sure it will help?"

"I think it will," I nodded lightly in encouragement.

"In my former life I was a psychiatrist," she said.

"A noble profession," I commented.

She smiled and chuckled, but the smile didn't reach her eyes. "I used to think so," she continued. "I was straight out of college. Fresh faced and naive. I was barely twenty-two. I wanted to save the world with my compassion. So I joined a small free health clinic in the inner city. It was such fulfilling work for a time. I could tell when I was helping people. I specialized in child psychiatry, so I worked with mostly children. Quickly the work started to become overwhelming. There were so many children that came through the clinic and some began to slip through the cracks. I just couldn't keep up. On most cases I just began calling Social Services over to have them take some of the pressure off. I went in one day to put in my notice. The work was killing me and I needed out."

Valerie took a deep breath. I leaned forward and patted her knee to show comfort. She smiled back at me.

"I went in and right away I knew something was wrong," she said and her eyes seemed to glaze over. "I'd entered through the back door, which was my normal entry. The lobby was empty and no one was at the front desk. For as long as I could remember there was always someone in that clinic. It was never empty. Before I could turn to leave, someone came up behind me and hit me in the back of the head."

Valerie swallowed hard as she continued.

"When I came to, he was on top of me," she said. "He had dragged me to my office and was ripping at my clothes. I froze. He was yelling at me about taking away his daughter. How he was going to give me what I deserved for making his wife leave him and sending his daughter into the system. It wasn't until he was pushing himself into me that I began fighting and screaming. After he finished, I curled into a ball and sobbed for I don't know how long. I found out later that he'd called in a bomb threat, and in the amount of time that it took the clinic to clear out and the police to get there he'd been able to hide and ambush me, unaware of the situation."

I stared in shock.

"The guilt was crushing," she described. "That was the worst part. I went over that day over and over again. I'd had to look up the daughter's case file to even remember her name. He'd only said her first name, and I just couldn't remember the case. It took me a long time to come to terms with what happened. I struggled deeply with depression and even admitted myself into a psych ward. It took two years and a ton of therapy for me to finally accept what happened. That there wasn't anything I could have done to prevent it. I never forgave him, but I finally forgave myself. It hurt, but I was ready to move on. I was ready to live again. That was my choice."

"I'm so sorry," I wiped at the tears that coursed unchecked down my face. "I had no idea."

"Of course not," she gave a watery laugh. "Why would you? I worked very hard to make sure I don't look like a victim. I am a survivor."

"Well you did an incredible job, you're gorgeous."

A surprised and genuine laugh escaped Valerie. It seemed to startle her.

"Now you know my deep, dark secret," she said. "You'll have to share yours some time."

Standing she walked toward the door and this time I didn't stop her. Before she made her exit, she turned and looked back at me.

"I've found that even in the darkest of places," she said quietly. "There is always a way to find the light. Even if you have to create it yourself."

To punctuate the point she held out her hand and held a tiny ball of fire. Then in a blink it was gone and so was she.

Standing on wobbly legs, I left the music room to find my way back the library. I needed to do some research.

It took over an hour to locate the one legitimate book from the index cards. Thankfully there was more than one reading space in the library so when I did find it, I didn't have too far to walk to curl up in a nice comfy chair next to a fire. I wondered idly who tended the large number of fires I'd seen in my short time there. Shrugging off the thought, I opened the book and began reading. I was tired enough that I fell asleep soon after the first page.

My dreams always took me to exotic places I'd never thought to visit. I had been so focused on school to earn my education and then my job that it was impossible to justify such an expense.

Currently I was on a white sandy beach where I lay in the sun, stretched naked on a large light colored blanket. Next to me, Alexandar lay, looking at me with a light I couldn't fathom. It spoke of deep connection and an affection I'd never known. When he smiled I smiled back.

A cloud crossed the sun and blocked the light. I didn't think anything about it until the wind picked up and the warmth I'd felt moments ago disappeared. I looked off towards where the sun had been and a dark void now occupied the space. It was a living thing, this darkness. I looked back to where Alexandar had been and found the space empty. Terrified, I rose and began to run as pelting rain slammed into the beach. The waves crashed violently on the beach, ripping at my legs as I ran through the surf. I stumbled and fell as a wall of water washed over me. Struggling to breathe, the salt claimed my lungs for their own. Sputtering, I clawed at the sand attempting to find purchase. The water was relentless, the earth sucked at my body to keep it from moving, the warmth and security of the sun had abandoned me. I was alone and I was going to die.

Bolting upright, I dropped the book from my lap and gasped for air. I coughed up salt water and sputtered. A blanket was dropped around me and I shuddered at the sudden warmth. I was soaked to the bone and so cold it hurt. My lungs screamed with the new influx of air like I'd stuck a hot poker down my throat to burn them. I fell to the floor but was scooped up and brought next to the fire. The warmth was too much and I struggled lightly while someone rubbed my arms. Slowly, as my teeth chattering and body shaking subsided, I realized that someone was whispering to me. It was another language but it sounded familiar somehow. I couldn't place the dialect.

Looking up I saw that it was Alexandar. His eyes were closed and he seemed to be shaking as well, though not from the cold that I so obviously felt. He kept repeating the same phrase over and over.

"Ormsa an locht, is mise is ciontach leis," he said. "Ormsa an locht, is mise is ciontach leis."

"What does that mean?" I wondered aloud as my shaking and chill halted altogether.

Startled, his eyes popped open. When he looked at me it seemed as if time itself stopped. I couldn't hear the crackle of the fire behind me anymore. All I could see was his eyes. In them lived regret and desperation. He pulled me close and hugged me tight to his body. It was then that I realized his hair was wet.

"How did we get wet?" I asked but before I could seek an answer his lips covered mine and all thought of what had just happened slipped away.

His lips were rough and demanding. It was all I could do to answer their searching. Electricity shot through my body and I struggled to free my arms from the constricting blanket. He pulled back lightly and set his forehead on mine. I attempted to restart the kiss but was unable to maneuver around my confinement. His breaths came in raspy spasms as if he'd just run several miles without water. The way my body was straining and shuddering I could understand his heavy breathing, especially if he was trying to resist the pull that I felt. It was strong and undeniable.

"I can't," he dropped me from his lap suddenly and walked several feet away to give himself space. I wriggled out of the blanket but did not leave the comforting warmth of the fire behind me. My clothes still clung to my body as if I'd jumped into a lake fully clothed. I watched Alexandar warily as he paced the small length of the reading area, mumbling to himself.

"You couldn't have slept in your room," he said under his breath. "You had to fall asleep in the one place that isn't protected. Why couldn't you be normal? Why do you feel safe around books?"

"What were you saying earlier?" I asked.

"What?" He paused his pacing, seeming to realize I was still there.

"What does 'Ormsa an locht, is mise is ciontach leis'," I repeated the phrase back to him. "Mean?"

"What?" He seemed embarrassed.

"Roughly translated it means, 'It's my fault'." Came a disembodied voice from the stacks.

I turned and frowned from the place I'd heard the voice come from.

"Shut it, Book," Alexandar spit.

"Who was that?" I turned back to him.

"Uh..." Alexandar sighed and rolled his neck around while massaging his temples. "Some books in the library are enchanted."

"What does that mean?" I asked, my head starting to hurt.

"It means that some of the books in the library will answer questions you ask them if the answer is contained within their volume." Another disembodied voice called from a different stack.

"So if I ask questions aloud, I will gain answers just by being near volumes that have been enchanted?"

"Yes," several voices answered.

"Hmm," I processed that. "How many books in the library are enchanted?"

When no disembodied voice answered I looked at Alexandar.

"No one knows," he said. "Though I would be careful with the questions you ask because you may not always like the answer. And the books cannot always be trusted."

"What does that mean?"

"That there are books from all over the world in here, written by hundreds of thousands of different authors," he said. "Do you trust everything you read?"

"If it is from a reputable source and has factual evidence of its findings," I said.

"Then keep that in mind when you ask questions," he said vaguely. "Let's get you cleaned up."

"That reminds me," I remarked. "How did we get wet?"

"You don't remember?" Alexandar asked me.

"I remember that I was having a nightmare," I said. "And that you woke me. Did you dump water on me? In the future, shaking or calling my name would suffice."

"I didn't dump water on you," he chuckled lightly.

The sound send a charge up my spine as I saw the grin wink across his face for a split second.

"Then how?"

"You were attacked," he told me.

"How is that possible?"

"It's hard to explain," he said. "When you sleep you leave yourself vulnerable. You believe you're safe. Unless you take certain precautions you can be pulled into another realm, or what some refer to as a dreamscape. If you are trained you can defend yourself within that dreamscape utilizing the things around you. But you are not trained."

"Like lucid dreaming?" I wondered.

"Similar," he said. "Except these dreamscapes can have deadly consequences that follow your body in reality."

"But that's not possible," I said as we continued walking.

"And talking books are?" He scoffed. "You have a skewed idea of reality when you pick some things to believe and others to reject."

"I mean," I said. "It's not possible because I can't die in my own subconscious."

"How do you know?" He asked. "There have been hundreds of studies on dreaming and the sleep walking that can be deadly associated with it."

"That's true I suppose," I nodded. "But why would I be wet with seawater? I don't know that it's possible that I sleep walked all the way to New York Bay."

"That's a puzzle isn't it?"

Alexandar walked me all the way to a new doorway and showed me to a room. It wasn't as large as other rooms I'd seen but it was more than serviceable.

"I should have shown this to you earlier. I apologize that you felt the need to sleep in the library. In the future please sleep here." Alexandar said. "We've taken precautions in all of our rooms so that attacks are near impossible. Tomorrow I will teach you to protect yourself."

"Umm..." I was never at a loss for words, but watching him turn to leave left me speechless. He paused and waited for me to continue. I wanted to ask him about his story, but I was still reeling from what Valerie had revealed.

"Yes?"

"Never mind," I said. "Thank you."

After he left I stripped off my still damp clothes and crawled under the covers stretched tight on the full sized bed. Quickly I fell dreamlessly into sleep.

 I woke to darkness and for a moment I was disoriented. My loft was never this dark. Then it dawned on me. I sat up and rolled out of bed, where I found a candle and matches on a stand next to the bed. Striking one I touched the tip to the wick and watched as it caught then waved my hand to extinguish the match.

Across the room next to the door I found a neatly folded pile of clothes. A modest pair of jeans, t-shirt and hiking boots. I wondered idly if we would be hiking today. As I dressed I found the book I had begun to read yesterday under the pile. When I was done dressing I took the book and walked into the hallway to find some coffee. I felt groggy and a bit misty minded. I needed to clear the cobwebs.

The dining room was just as I'd left it the day before, except there were different foods available. I wondered again who put all of this together. My thoughts were swept away as I heard quiet conversation. After helping myself to the food I wandered to the table and took my seat. Though I could have sworn I heard conversation, no one was at the table. With no one to offend I opened my book and read as I ate. I smiled to myself, my mother had hated the habit.

The first page held a bunch of signatures, which I thought was odd. Did some people just want to sign the books they'd read? It made sense in a way, I supposed. With as many books that were in the library it may be a breadcrumb of sorts, something to leave behind confirming your literary journey. There was a cup of pens on a desk nearby so I grabbed one and sat back down. I wrote my name under the list and watched in awe as it glowed lightly then sealed itself on the page. I ran my thumb over it and what should have smudged held firm as if it had been written here hundreds of years ago. The book shuddered at my touch and began flipping pages to the exact middle of the volume, where a small ball of light glowed and pulsed like the beat of a heart.

"Greetings Tabitha, Daughter of Air," it intoned.

"Daughter of Air?" I asked.

The book paused and the pulse beat quickly like fluttering pages.

"There are several references to the Daughter of Air in this volume," it said. "Be more specific in your query."

I furrowed my brows as I watched the light pulse. This must be one of the enchanted books.

"What is the definition of Daughter of Air," I asked.

The pages flipped nearly to the front and the voice recited the section I was looking for.

"The Sons and Daughters of Air are descendants from the original Elementals formed at the beginning of time."

The pages were filled with beautiful script and pictures.

"What are the Elementals?"

"The Elementals are the Sons and Daughters of Earth, Air, Fire and Water."

"That doesn't make any sense," I stated as if to give a rebuttal. "Ok. Are the Sons and Daughters direct descendants of each other as its title suggests?"

"The Sons and Daughters are not direct descendants of each other."

"Why is it not hereditary?"

"The Sons and Daughters usually do not live long enough to procreate."

That answer took me aback.

"Why are the lifespans so short?" I asked, confused.

"The Elementals are warriors in the fight against the Void." It said as if that answered my question fully.

"What is the Void and why do the Elementals fight it?"

"The Void is the absence of life and light. The Elementals fight against the forces of the Void to protect the Earth, where the Elements and its servants live in relative harmony."

"What is the difference between Elementals and the Elements?"

"Elementals are the human vessel for the Elements," it said. "Elementals, in return for being the sole guardian for its Element, are allowed it's full or near full power."

"Like magic?" I asked.

"There are several references to magic in this volume," it said. "Please be more specific in your query."

"Uh..." I hesitated trying to best describe what I wanted to know. "Is the power of the Elements the same as magic?"

"Magic is not real," it said. "But the power of the Elements are. With the power to control your given element, you can do things that will trick humans into believing that magic is real. Which is why the myth surrounding magic exists. Magic and Elemental Powers are not the same."

My brow furrowed. Every fantasy book I'd ever read insisted that if you could control the Elements then it was through magic. But I suppose magic is subjective in a way. Giving a name to something that explains a connection when there are no facts to substantiate it. Like the air.

"How are the Elementals chosen?" I asked without even thinking about it.

"The Sons and Daughters are chosen by their respective elements at a moment when they choose life over death and are proven worthy of the power bestowed upon them."

"What..." Before I could finish my question a movement to my right had me looking up. Alexandar sat down with a plate of food, then Valerie across from me with a heaping mound of food and Chauncy followed to my left.

"Don't let us disturb your studies," Valerie said as she began devouring her food.

"My mother beat it into me that it was terrible table manners to read at the table," I said.

"I'm so sorry," Valerie blanched as she dropped the fork she'd held, where it clattered noisily to her plate.

Valerie and Chauncy's dire backgrounds had me realizing that they may take my words literally.

"No, I'm sorry," I said quickly. "I was using the figure of speech, not the literal one. My mother didn't beat me."

"Ah," Valerie's face pinkened as she breathed deep and she sat back, picking at her food.

"So why are you here?" Alexandar asked into the awkward silence.

This somehow achieved a higher sense of tension than I had thought possible.

"Alexandar..." Chauncy chided.

"What?" He asked indignantly. "You all have shared yours with her, maybe it's time she shared her life and death story."

"It's alright," I said to calm the tension that seemed to be crackling across the table.

"You don't have to share it until you're ready," Valerie said with an encouraging smile.

"It's alright," I repeated. "My story isn't as painful as what's been shared with me so far."

Chauncy settled back into his chair with a final glare at Alexandar, which he returned easily as it seemed to be his homeostasis.

"My sister died," though it happened what seemed like a lifetime ago, my face crumpled and it suddenly became hard to breathe. Just the reminder that Samantha was not part of this world anymore was shattering. It hurt, but it hurt a little less each day. When I regained control of my emotions again I wiped my nose and continued.

"She was the only friend I'd ever had," I blew my nose with a tissue Valerie handed me. "My mother wasn't abusive in the sense that she hit me, but she never truly accepted me. No matter what I did, for whatever reason, she couldn't love me. But she loved my sister. I envied that. My sister never rubbed it in my face, she consoled me the best way she knew how. We were extremely close. I've never been able to make friends easily, so she was my sole comfort when I needed to speak with someone or just to have any sort of human contact. My father was absent, so he either didn't notice or didn't care. When she died it felt like my entire life had been torn apart. I stood near a busy street corner during rush hour and I thought about just falling into traffic. But I didn't. I chose to keep living."

"There are many types of abuse," Valerie said. "Yours may have not been physical, but the wounds are just as real. And the loss of your sister is never something to be taken lightly, especially if you two were as close as you say."

I looked over at Alexandar who seemed uncomfortable.

"Some say the Elements choose you at your worst moment in life," Chauncy said looking at Alexandar. "At the point when you prove your loyalty to life."

"That's not always true though," Alexandar said darkly as he stood. "Sometimes you have worse moments, unthinkable pain and torment after you're chosen."

I watched as he left the room, leaving his plate untouched.

"He lost someone very close to him," Valerie said. "He's still trying to cope."

"Oh," I said.

"Maybe you should go after him," Chauncy suggested with a grin.

"I'm not sure if I'm the right person to comfort him right now," I said into my plate.

"He's going topside," Chauncy said. "You need to see it anyway."

Nodding, I stood as Chauncy gave me directions to the hatch. The tunnels were more cavernous in some places and the main hallway always seemed to shift to the right, giving the impression that it was a giant ring. Finally in a particularly large room with four different sized thrones, I found a ladder that went up. I heard a clank and an odd howling sound echo down, though I couldn't see the end. It confirmed that Alexandar had gone this way, so I followed.

I climbed and climbed. I climbed until my muscles began shaking and I was so far off the ground I was a little afraid I would get stuck. In response to my fear, I felt the air stir around me like a warm encouraging caress. It pushed me to keep moving, and finally I found the hatch. It was round and metal, similar to what I'd seen on submarines. Since it was unlocked I didn't have to turn the large wheel, so I just pushed it open. Immediately the wind whipped at my hair as I climbed out. It felt like a wind tunnel. Oddly though, as soon as I was standing on the ground the air seemed to move around rather than against me. Excitement seemed to dance around me in near visible waves. I turned to muscle the hatch but it closed without much effort. This wind explained the howling I'd heard.

I saw Alexandar stomping toward me. He seemed to be saying
something but I couldn't hear him over the roar of wind. As I
wished for the wind to die down so I could hear him, it did. The
wild current of air ceased. I looked around and saw that there was a
circular bubble of calm surrounding us. There was a mountain
directly across from us and surrounding it were trees and shrubs
similar to the garden I'd seen in the music room with Alexandar.
Everything was green and lovingly tended. The plants grew and
flourished.

"Why are you here?" His yell broke the cone of silence.

"Is this my power?" I wondered aloud.

"I repeat," he said. "What. Are you. Doing here?"

He punctuated his sentence with pauses, I would assume to
convey a sense of intense frustration. I wasn't sure how to
approach him so I just started with honesty.

"Chauncy said it might be a good idea for me to see the roof,"
I said. Ok, half honesty.

"Of course he did," Alexandar threw up his hands and turned
away from me.

It was starting to feel really hot in this bubble, I was starting to
sweat.

"Can you tell me your story?" I asked.

"No," he said. "Not right now."

"Why?" I asked.

"Because I'm still living it," he snapped.

"Ok," I said. "Then can you teach me what you were planning
to the other day?"

Sweat was really starting to drip down my face and back. I
was starting to feel weak and drawn.

"Fine," he said hunching his shoulder.

Turning around he looked at me again and immediately a look
of concern entered his face.

"What is wrong with you?" he asked, striding forward. He
grabbed my arms as I collapsed. "Release your element, stupid."

"I don't know what that means," I stated wearily. My words
slurred as if I'd drunk a glass of wine too quickly before eating.

"Stop asking it to create this bubble," he shook me.

"I still don't understand," my eyes were getting heavy.

With a growl, he threw me over his shoulder and ran into the torrent of wind and under the cover of a nearby cave. Almost immediately my strength returned and I gasped for breath. My muscles shook as if I'd worked every single muscle in my body rigorously. It took a long time before the spasms in my body stopped. He sat on the ground and cradled me while I attempted to pull myself together.

"What was that?" I asked once I was steady again.

"That was you being stupid," he said.

"Ok," I waited for him to be more forthcoming. When he wasn't I asked. "Can you be clearer on how?"

"You asked your element to work against itself," he said. "That takes a lot of energy from you in return."

"I did no such thing," I tried to rise and fell back into his lap shuddering.

"You could have died," he said very quietly.

"What?" Shocked, I looked up at him.

The small amount of light that was provided from the exterior showed the planes and angles of his face. He leaned back against the cave wall with his eyes closed, breathing heavily.

"What's your element?" I asked curious.

"Earth," he said without opening his eyes.

"How do you work against your element and make it take energy?" I asked.

"You ask it to work against itself," he said. "Like changing the natural flow of a river, or tides. Forcing a volcanic eruption to stop. Creating a massive earthquake or telling the wind not to blow."

"Working against nature itself," I said.

He nodded and looked down at me.

"You could have died," he repeated, more forcefully.

"Well it's not like I've had a teacher so far," I said grumpily. "You all have kind of had me figuring it all out for myself."

"You don't think it's real," he said, his face forming stony lines. "So what do you care?"

Alexandar stood, dumping me unceremoniously on my butt.

"Oof," I rubbed my rear end and wobbly got to my feet.

"How can I convince you that this is real?" He asked. "What can I do?"

Before I could answer, he stepped forward and kissed me. Electricity felt like it shot from my fingers and toes. I wrapped my arms around his neck to pull him closer. He pushed me against the wall and ran his hands up and down my back lighting little fires wherever they touched. My heartbeat thudded against my ribs, threatening to break out of my chest.

Alexandar pressed against me and a noise I could only describe as a purr escaped me at the pressure. Waves and waves of pleasure were crashing against me. I'd never felt anything like this before. How could this be in my mind? The thought had me freezing and pulling away. He stopped his onslaught with what seemed like thinly chained restraint. He was breathing just as heavily as I was and let me slide to the ground. I pulled my legs to my chest and began to rock.

"What?" he said between gasps. "What?"

He tried to touch me again, but I recoiled.

"Tabitha," he said my name like a whisper. "What did I do?"

"You made me believe," I said. Tears cascaded down my cheeks.

"It was that easy?" Alexandar seemed to scoff.

"Yes," I said. "It's not that hard when you've never been loved before."

"What do you mean?" He sat down directly in front of me.

"Never mind," I said quickly. "I need to see my nephews. I need to find them."

"Ok," he said. "I'll go with you."

The old insecurities began setting in. The horror of everything that I'd done over the last few days tore at me. My face flamed. I'd basically asked him to have sex with me. He's seen me naked. I treated these kind people as if they were a means to an end for my sanity. What must they think of me? I needed to leave. Shutting down, I ran from the cave. From Alexandar. He called after me but I didn't want him to follow. I did my best not to ask my element to work against itself but asked it to keep him from following me at the moment. Just enough to give me a head start.

I wasn't very athletic so I needed all the help I could get. When I felt the now familiar sweat on my back, I thanked the element and let it know I was fine now. This time I could feel the severing of energy. It was a physical pull, like slack on a rope. I could feel it around me now that I was looking for it. Instead of being anchored, I now had room to move. I ran as far as I could for as long as I could. The physical exertion had my skin damp again, but it was a different kind of sweat, born from work rather than pain. Exhausted, I sat under a tree. My lungs burned with the pressure from running. I gulped air, trying to calm myself. The pain in my muscles and lungs seemed so real. But how was that possible? How was all of this real? It couldn't be. But what other explanation did I have?

Maybe the problem wasn't that this might be real, but that I wanted nothing more than for this to be reality. I wanted to be special. I wanted to be loved. I wanted friends who liked me for me. That's why this couldn't possibly be real. I wanted this too much and it was exactly what I needed to overcome my grief.

"Of course it's not real," a hissing voice came from above me.

Looking up I saw movement on one of the branches. It moved like a snake but as it came closer, wrapping its long sinewy body around the tree, I could see that it had patterns like a patchwork quilt, eyes that glowed bright blue and sharp, dagger looking teeth. Its tongue, as it flicked in and out, looked like a human's split in two and extended.

"Why would you think anyone could like you?" It hissed out a chuckle.

I scrambled back from the tree as it attempted to wrap around my shoulder.

"What are you?" I shuddered as it flicked its disgustingly out of place tongue at me between the sharp teeth.

"I'm a friend who wants to tell you the truth," it hissed.

"A friend?" I scoffed.

"Yesssss," it said. "I'm just confirming what you already think. Why would he love you? It must be fake. It's either staged or someone is attempting to undermine your credibility. Think of all your scholastic work, down the drain."

The true echo of my thoughts was unnerving.

"I worked so hard," I said as if in a trance.

"You sacrificed so much to be more than you were," it hissed hypnotically. "And now the universe wants to give you everything for nothing? Unlikely."

"Yes, unlikely," I repeated. My head was fuzzy and its body looked so comfortable. The patchwork quilt slithered closer and wrapped around me, and squeezed me like a comforting hug.

"No!" The trance was broken as the teeth grew larger, directly in front of my face.

Alexandar jumped from the surrounding foliage and grabbed my ankle as I tumbled backward. I fell and swung from the edge of the world. I looked around me and screamed. There was nothing. No ground, no sky. It was a sea of clouds. As I swung upside down the snake-thing squeezed harder and opened its jaws again. A rock came zooming out of nowhere and hit the back of its neck, knocking it loose. The thing screamed a very human sounding scream and dropped away like fog in the night. I watched as it swirled downward toward the clouds.

Alexandar struggled to pull me upward. My head hit dirt behind me as he attempted to swing me. I saw behind me that there was a giant mountain of dirt, as if someone had pulled this jungle forest up by its roots, just like a clump of grass.

"A little help please?" Alexandar huffed.

"Right," I said. Using the current air around me, I thought about it changing direction just enough to help rather than hinder his attempted rescue.

Suddenly, I was thrust upward and into Alexandar. We slid backward on the dirt with another *oof.*

"Are you ok?" Alexandar asked quickly. He patted down my body as I lay on top of him, looking for breaks.

"I'm fine," I said. "Thank you."

"Good," he said, his face changing from worry to rage in the blink of an eye. "Because I'm going to beat you senseless."

He pushed up and took me with him. Pulling my arm we moved away from the edge of the world. I looked back wistfully, wishing I could study it.

"Where are we?" I asked. "I just thought we were underground somewhere."

"Our Sanctuary," he said.

"It's a floating island?" I asked.

"In a way," he said.

"Where are we going?" I asked, pulling back slightly.

"You need a crash course in how to defend yourself," he said then looked back for a moment. "And I'm going to give it to you."

He was swearing in a language I didn't understand, a long unbroken stream of muttered curses. The tone and tenor lent to the idea that they were swears with the way they spat out of his mouth. Occasionally he would look back at me and ask me a question in that same language as if I were going to answer. When I didn't the swearing would start again.

Alexandar pulled me toward the hatch. As we neared it I wondered how he expected to climb the ladder while keeping hold of my hand. My question was answered when he opened the hatch one handed then proceeded to pick me up and jump down the hole. I didn't even have time to scream - immediately we came into contact with solid ground. After he secured the hatch we lowered like an elevator until we hit the bottom. The ground at the bottom was completely unbroken, as if there hadn't been a little earthen elevator just seconds ago. Without pause Alexandar continued on his quest. Still cursing, though it seemed like he was losing steam, we walked a short time before entering a bedroom.

After closing and locking the door he finally freed my hand and continued to pace. He ran his hand through his hair, making it even more disheveled. The loose curls began to poke out at odd angles and it made me smile to watch him trying to reign in his frustration.

"What?" Alexandar halted abruptly and stared at me.

"Um..." I tried to hide my smile, but failed miserably.

"You think this is funny?" He asked, walking toward until his face was right next to mine. "You think that this is a joke?"

"No," I sobered. "I was just wondering if maybe your element should have been fire, since your temper seems hard for you to control."

"Well," he said losing his bite. "It's not. Do you know what could have happened up there? You don't do you. Do you even think it's real?"

"Yes," I said.

That seemed to make him pause.

"You do?" He asked.

"Yes," I huffed out a breath. "I've accepted my situation. But that means I need to find my nephews, they could be in danger."

"Ok, then," he said, then seemed to hesitate. "Is it because we...."

"No. The deciding factor was that... thing. It was trying so hard to convince me that this wasn't real. If I were in a delusion because I needed a mental break, why would an enemy tell me my experiences were false? In reality I would trust no one but my sister telling me something wasn't real," I told him. "That snake thing telling me that all my worst fears were real, was what tipped the scales for me."

"Well," Alexandar seemed slightly disappointed.

"I apologize for my convoluted explanation," I shrugged. "It is difficult to explain my thought process."

If I still believed I was delusional I would have told him our kiss had been a tipping point for me and that I'd never felt like this before with anyone because I was inexperienced. But I knew it was all real now so the old doubts began cramming themselves in. I cleared my throat and shifted awkwardly.

"Once you've mastered protecting yourself, then we can go see your nephews," he said.

"Mhmm," I said absently.

I knew that my focus should be on my nephews, but I was having trouble concentrating at his nearness. I wished longingly for the strength to tell him how I felt. I could see myself slipping back into the mousey shell and I loathed it. How was I supposed to act now? I had other people's feelings to consider. I just really wanted to tell him how attractive his messy hair was, how much I wanted to fix it and run my own hands through it. How much I wanted to kiss him. The fear I would feel at his inevitable rejection when he found someone else better, prettier, and more confident than me.

I looked up from my own musings to see him studying me.

"What?" I demanded more forcefully than I'd meant. I was just so frustrated at myself.

"Why are you angry?" Alexandar's brows drew together.

"I'm not angry," I huffed. Crossing my arms I noticed a smile tug at the corners of his mouth.

"What's funny?" I wanted to know. His obvious amusement at the situation was pushing my buttons and I didn't like being laughed at.

"Nothing," he coughed trying to cover his laughter. "Nothing."

"There seems to be something tickling your fancy, or why would you be laughing at me?"

"'Tickling your fancy?'" Alexandar laughed outright.

I flexed my jaw and turned to leave. A hand on my arm stopped me.

"Wait," Alexandar continued to chuckle as I shrugged off his hand. "Come on. Ok, I'm sorry."

"About what?" I brushed at his hand on my arm like it was a bug.

"I'm not laughing at you," he sobered.

"I'm sure," I frowned at the hand that still rested on my arm until he removed it and raised both arms in surrender.

"Alright, alright," he said. "I laughed a little but who says 'tickle your fancy'?"

With a sigh of disgust I turned to leave again as his voice rose in laughter again.

"Don't you want to learn why you were drenched in salt water yesterday?" He managed to get out between chuckles. My curiosity was the only thing that would have stopped me.

"Do you miss your friend?" I asked. "Is that why this is hard for you to accept me?"

"Who told you that?" Immediately the easy grin was gone, replaced by the anger that always seemed close to the surface.

I shrugged and watched him pull himself together. He looked like I had just punched him in the gut.

"You want to hear my story?" He asked. Though his face was set in angry lines, his voice sounded more tired than anything. I nodded.

"Fine," he said curtly. "Then we get to work."

Slowly, he walked to an oversized leather chair and sat. Eyes closed, he seemed to gather himself before speaking.

"The previous Air Elemental was my sister," he said with a great expulsion of breath. It seemed like a great weight had been lifted from his shoulders, but the words seemed foreign when they tumbled from his mouth, as if he couldn't stand their taste.

"She and I were chosen at the same time," he said. "We were twins. We had done everything together since we were born. It was always a race for us, a competition. We grew up in the slums of Ireland. Slept in some nasty places, but we always watched out for each other. I don't want to go into the sad details that had us choosing, but it was not in a good way. We chose each other, we chose life and we fought. Chauncy came for us and he showed us what life could be. We've been with Chauncy since we were ten."

"What happened to her?" I asked.

"The same thing that almost happened to you," he said. "She got cocky and thought she could take the Void on. An agent overcame her mental shield and she died. Do you understand now how serious this is?"

"Yes," I nodded. "What was the thing that attacked me?"

"It was a Doppelganger," he said. "The same type of monster that attacked you in the dream sleep at your townhouse. They work for the Agents of the Void. There are four of them, just like there are four of us. Only they didn't choose life, they chose death and power. Albeit, possibly with some pushing from the Void."

"Why did it look like that?"

"Doppelgangers have a hard time taking the form of anything living, so they imitate," he stretch his neck. "But there is always a flaw. Some are easier to spot than others if they aren't as adept at imitation."

"Like the man I saw after I was Chosen." I said, more to myself, thinking of the man with shark-like teeth that had pushed me into traffic as soon as I'd chosen to live.

"You saw him right after you were Chosen?" Alexandar leaned forward, suddenly very interested.

"Yeah, he pushed me into traffic," I said. "I know now that I was being selfish in my grief, but just as I'd chosen life he appeared in front of me and I fell into traffic. Then everything just stopped. Time literally held still. I got up and followed the sound of footsteps and found a card that turned into a dandelion. Can you see why I was doubting my sanity at the beginning of this adventure?"

"Impossible," Alexandar whispered.

"What?" I asked.

"Even for us it's difficult to find someone right before they are Chosen," he said. "When someone is chosen it creates a bond. We can feel each other as if we've been tied together. You probably haven't felt it yet because we haven't left the island, but it's real. However, we can't find the fellow Elementals until they make their choice, which is why we weren't there immediately to help you. The question I have is why an Agent of the Void knew where to find you before we did."

"But if it wasn't you," I said. "Then who stopped time and left a dandelion?"

"That's a something I'd like to know as well," he frowned. "But before we can start research, you need to learn how to protect your mind."

"Hmm," I nodded, still thinking about my first day as a Chosen Guardian.

I stretched in the sand and soaked up the sun. This time I had a bathing suit on, but Alexandar still lay next to me smiling.

"Is this your idea of paradise?" he asked.

"No," I said. "But it's nice. How did we get here?"

"I took you here with my mind," he said. "You need to break free of my control."

"But this is so nice," I said as the sun beat down on my skin. "I've never been to a beach like this before."

"Fine," he said. "We could lounge here for years if you wanted. But then who's going to protect your nephews?"

I opened one eye and peaked at him, playfully sticking out my tongue.

"How do I break your control?" I asked.

"One way," Alexandar told me. "Is to break the attacker's concentration. Another is to kill them. These worlds are so expansive that it can be hard to find the attacker unless they make themselves known."

"So what if I can't find them?" I asked.

"Then you need backup," he smiled at me and my heart skipped a beat. "Call one or all of us in."

"How?"

"You did it before with me at the beach, though that may not have been your intention. Just by wanting someone there, you can usually bring them in. Your element is powerful, if left unchecked it will carry out your every unspoken action and word. You need to be very intentional in your thoughts."

"That seems exhausting," I frowned.

"It can be," Alexandar nodded. "So that's why I find a quiet place and tell my element just to support me in my thoughts. Then it has an action to concentrate on while I just let my mind wander. I can create all sorts of worlds that way."

"Was that what you were doing the other night in the music room?" I rolled over to face him.

"Yes," he said. I watched him pick up his arm then let it drop.

I scooted a little closer and watched him struggle with himself before making his face a blank mask. I moved my hand to his bare chest and felt the heartbeat, clear as day. Everything felt so real that we could have really been at the beach. His skin felt warm and grainy from the sand. At my touch, his heartbeat picked up and his breathing quickened. He didn't move, but I could tell he wanted to. I wanted to move my hand so I did. That was the one thing that was different than the real world. Even if I had reservations about doing something I still did it here because I wanted to. That was really saying something about Alexandar's strength of will.

"What are you thinking about?" I asked as his breathing turned ragged.

"My sister," the confession caught me by surprise and the illusion dropped away.

"I'm not sure how to take that," I said as we sat in his bedroom again.

"Well you broke my concentration that's for sure," he frowned at me. "My entire focus was split on continuing the illusion and not..."

His voice trailed off and he coughed.

"So unfortunately I couldn't keep from telling you my thoughts." He said after a moment.

"Do you think of her when you look at me?" I asked.

"Yes," he squeezed his eyes shut and ran his hands through his hair again. "But not the way you're thinking. She is never far from my mind. I miss her every day. Shall we try again?"

I put my hand on his knee and smiled lightly when he looked up at me.

"I understand," I told him.

"I know you do," he put his hand over mine and squeezed.

Over the next hour we went back and forth. He showed me how to protect my mind from someone entering it when I was in public by using my element as a mental shield. He explained that it wasn't foolproof and that if I needed it maintained I wouldn't be able to do a myriad of tasks as well. The Elementals power wasn't infinite, but it wouldn't get tired or need a rest. You could transfer power from the tasks to other things. We went through a large number of scenarios and it actually became fun trying to outwit him. Though it was only an hour in real time it seemed like weeks of training. He even began showing me how to fight with my element. I was excited to try it out.

When we were done training we were both covered in muck from our various travels. Alexandar had explained to me that this travel was a form of astral projection. With every projection you brought something back with you, good or bad. So it was always a good idea to cleanse afterward, body and mind.

We both entered the hot springs, this time with a bathing suit on and enjoyed the cleansing. As I floated through the water, much like the island carrying us, a thought occurred to me.

"If we can't make the elements work against themselves indefinitely, how is this floating island possible?"

Finished, Alexandar was sitting on the side of the pool, watching as I floated.

"A few Elementals gave their lives so that the future ones could have a permanent sanctuary," he yawned and stretched, then leaned back while keeping his feet in the water. "The gift of their life force was enough of a boost to move the island into the stratosphere where it's relatively easy to be kept afloat. We orbit the earth, like the moon. Even though the Elementals didn't know the specific science on where to move the island to make it easy to be kept afloat the Elements knew, so when they were asked the

Elements complied the best they knew how. This all came at great cost to the Elementals that asked. So it's actually a very small drain on us to keep it afloat."

"What happens when one, or all, of the Elementals die?" I wanted to know.

"The Elements can maintain the drift alone," he replied. "But not for long."

"If all the Elementals die at once," I wondered aloud. "How do they find out about their calling?"

"That hasn't happened in a long time," he yawned again. "But the legend says that the Elements can take human form for forty-eight hours before its life source is depleted and something really bad happens. The myths and legends surrounding the Elements are varied and scattered. Some say they are the Titans from Roman and Greek mythology. Some say they are the faeries and dryads of the forest, rivers, and fires of Ireland. I prefer that one, of course."

Alexandar chuckled to himself, then sat up.

"Alright," he stood and held out a hand to me. "Time to feed the body and regroup with the others."

Once dry, we changed into clean clothes and walked into the dining room. I could feel the new comradery between us and I enjoyed it. Though I only plied him with inane mechanical questions he seemed to be more relaxed than I'd seen him. I kept sneaking looks at him to see if the angry boy would return. It was only a matter of time, but decided not to ask.

We sat down at what seemed to be our assigned seats and ate. As soon as I sat, my stomach rumbled and I ate everything on my plate in what seemed like moments. I sat back and groaned.

"Feel better?" Valerie asked as she and Chauncy sat down.

"Much," I chuckled. "I'm not sure I've eaten much since I've gotten here."

"Anything?" Alexandar looked down the table at the two of them.

"Nothing," Chauncy shook his head.

"That means trouble," Alexandar nodded. "Remind me to punch you later."

Chauncy just chuckled.

"It could just mean they're retreating," Valerie suggested.

"To what end?" Alexandar wanted to know. "You know they never rest, especially after they took one of ours."

The frown was back, I sighed inwardly.

"They must be planning something big," Alexandar looked at me. "Tell us the whole story about your choice."

I frowned back at him but complied. I told them about the man that pushed me, time stopping, and the dandelion.

"They found her first?" Chauncy seemed shocked. "Before she'd even chosen?"

"Yes." Alexandar nodded.

"How is that possible?" Valerie wanted to know. "We don't even have that capability."

"I don't know," Alexandar replied. "But I think I have an idea. Let's go to the library."

"Ok," Chauncy nodded and stood. "But Alexandar, does the Dandelion mean what I think it means?"

"I think so." At Alexandar's response, both Valerie and Chauncy seemed to get excited.

"What does it mean?" I asked.

"The Time Warden," Valerie responded, as if that was an answer to my question.

They left as one and I struggled to catch up.

"Wait," I said. "Who is the Time Warden?"

"According to everything we've read," Chauncy replied over his shoulder as we all walked toward the library, "He's the Fifth Elemental. Much revered and the least seen. No one knows why."

"Hmm," I said absently as I processed that while we entered the library, with its seemingly endless stacks of books and still charming entryway.

Turning right immediately rather than moving toward the giant rolodex, they all walked to a panel of books just inside. Right away I could tell these were painted on. Alexandar pushed it lightly and the panel swung open easily to reveal a round room with an oval table and four high backed wooden chairs. The backs rose tall and ended in a point that resembled each of our elements. Chauncy took the fire chair, Valerie to the water chair and Alexandar took the earth chair. This left the final chair for me, air.

"Close the door behind you," Alexandar waved his hand absently.

The regal command had the hair on the back of my neck rising in irritation. I complied but I was unhappy about it. As soon as the door was closed I sat in my chair. Chauncy and Alexandar occupied the points of the oval and Valerie smiled at me from across the table.

Alexandar stood and grabbed a book from the walls, which were lined floor to ceiling with shelves. Mainly books covered them, but there were also some Knick-Knacks here and there and of course, a fire place. I made a mental note to ask about the servants later. I had yet to see anyone clear a table or stoke a fire, but this place was so large and there were so many secret passages I could have easily missed them.

"Moira and I came across this in our studies," he said. "We thought to use it, but we hadn't had the chance to puzzle it out."

He brought the book over and laid it out on the table.

"It's a tool that the Elementals can create to track Potentials," he said. "But it takes an infusion of all five Elements so we thought it was bunk."

"Until now," Chauncy said and Alexandar nodded.

"Until now," Alexandar repeated.

"But how did they get a device like this?" Valerie asked. "We obviously didn't infuse anything."

"No clue," Alexandar said. "But this is the only reason I can think that they could be getting to potentials before us."

"How long has it been happening?" I asked.

"No telling, really," Chauncy replied.

"I don't remember an Agent attacking me before I was Chosen," Valerie replied. "But you and Moira were chosen before me. So you remember anything like that?"

"No," Alexandar frowned thoughtfully. "But we were in a war zone that day, so it would have been difficult to discern."

"Warzone?" I latched onto that word.

"Not important right now," Alexandar waved it away.

"But..." I began.

"We just assumed they were tracking us," Chauncy interrupted smoothly.

"But maybe they just hadn't gotten the hang of the device yet," Alexandar said.

"How many potentials do you think they ended before they even got to choose?" Valerie asked.

"That might be unlikely," Chauncy said. "Because technically they are a potential Agent as well."

"A potential Agent?" I asked.

"The same as we are Chosen, so are they," Valerie said. "But they choose differently."

"It takes a specific type of person to choose life for selfless reasons," said Chauncy. "Rather than selfish or self-serving reasons."

"Or death," Alexandar put in.

"Or death," Chauncy nodded. "Technically if you sacrifice yourself to save the many."

"Wait," I said. "Backup. Are you telling me that even if you choose life, you could still become an Agent of the Void?"

"Yes," Valerie nodded. "If you choose your life at the expense of another living being's would be a reason."

"As a guardian," Alexandar said gravely. "You can still become an Agent of the Void if there is a vacancy and you make a different choice later down the road. We aren't paragons, Tabitha. We are still human. We still need to choose Life every day for the right reasons."

"Has that ever happened before?" I asked.

The room got very quiet. Even the fire in the hearth seemed to hold its breath.

"Yes," Alexandar said, his face unusually devoid of emotion.

I looked around the table but the others seemed to be busy looking at the book still open on the table.

"Ok," I said, but before I could ask further I was interrupted again.

"So what are we going to do about it?" Valerie asked.

"Well we need to address something first," Alexandar jumped on the topic change. "Tabitha has family we need to protect."

"Alright," Chauncy stood up. "Let's saddle up."

They all stood and filed out the hidden door before I could get a word in edgewise. I sighed and rose to follow in their footsteps.

 I struggled to keep up with them as they took their twists and turns. It was glaringly obvious that they knew their way around this labyrinth and I was still new here. When they all suddenly stopped I nearly ran into Alexandar. They spread out in a line with a person sized break. I stepped in to fill that hole and looked to see what was ahead of me.

A doorframe stood before me, containing a knob-less door with an intricate compass carved into its wood. The N indicating North pointed to the top of the frame, where a beautifully crafted oak tree seemed to grow up the wall. The Eastern point held a picture of stormy seas, with waves that looked so realistic I could swear they moved when I didn't stare directly at them. The Southern point held flames that licked at the sides of the compass, tracing their way to the frame surrounding it. Finally, the Western point had swirls that closed the gap between Earth and Fire. It fed directly into the waves unbreaking across from it. The time it must have taken to craft something so amazing was nearly unimaginable.

"What is it?" I asked, awed.

"Our gateway to the lower world," Chauncy replied.

"How do we use it?" I asked.

"We use ours keys," Valerie leaned forward and showed me hers.

It was a small silver key she kept on a necklace with chips of blue sodalite at its bow. The short length was like a skeleton key. It had beautifully crafted metalwork twisted around it like vines. An anchor hung from the side like a charm.

"I don't have a key," I said.

"You do," Alexandar turned to me. "Every time a new Elemental is chosen the key makes its way back to its home."

Alexandar pointed to five tiny drawers, all in a row, to the left of the door. These too were created with the utmost care and precision. They mirrored their compass points with a tiny knob depicting the elements. I walked closer to inspect them, each had a corresponding colored gem like the one I saw in Valerie's key.

Moss agate, blue sodalite, red garnet and yellow citrine. The fifth one was obsidian, its knob depicted a dandelion. I went to touch that box and received a small shock. I pulled back quickly and stuck the injured fingers in my mouth. I heard chuckles from behind me.

"I'd just touch your own box if I were you," Chauncy laughed.

"Why?" I asked. "What happens?"

"You're always so curious," Alexandar shook his head. "Basically, there's a built in security alarm. Anyone who tries to touch another Elemental's box gets cautioned against it."

Frowning, I turned back to the drawers and considered trying to open the black one anyway. Shaking my head I decided that was for another day and opened my own box. There was the sound of a vacuum releasing and the feeling of the air stirring around me, as if the drawer were sealed. It opened easily and revealed a little yellow velvet bed where a key lay nestled. The yellow citrine chips winked from its head and looked near identical to Valerie's key. The main difference between the two was that the charm that hung from mine was a single feather. When I looked into the gem the color reminded me of wind flowing through a sea of wheat. The field was endless and breathtaking. I picked up the key and it was warm, as if it had been waiting for me. A delicate silver chain was linked and unraveled as I lifted it. I immediately put the chain around my neck and closed the drawer. With one last look at the fifth drawer I took my place back in the line facing the door.

"Now what?" I asked.

Alexandar sighed as if he'd been holding his breath. The others looked relieved.

"Is there something I'm missing?" I asked.

"No," Valerie said quickly. "We were just happy that it was there."

"There was a possibility that it wouldn't be?"

"The last time we saw it..." Valerie trailed off looking at Alexandar.

"Was on my sister," Alexandar finished.

"How did it get back here," I asked. "If none of you are the ones that returned it."

"We aren't entirely sure," Chauncy answered.

"How did you doubt the existence of a fifth element when there was a box?" I asked.

"We still thought it was a myth," Valerie explained. "We've never seen them."

"What is it," I wondered. "The fifth element, that is."

"Time," Chauncy said.

"We have competing theories about why they don't fight with us," Alexandar said. "The most prevalent is that they defend on a different plane."

"Whoa," I said. "Now you want me to buy into different dimensions?"

They nodded. It was an unsettling prospect.

"How..."

"Do you want to see your nephews or not?" Alexandar seemed to have lost patience with my endless stream of questions. I nodded.

"Ok then," he ran a hand through his messy hair and removed his key from under his shirt.

Approaching the doorway, he took the key and I watched as the stones began to glow. A tiny keyhole slid open where a knot in the oak tree used to be. He inserted the key, turned it and backed away. Next Valerie did the same with the Eastern waves. An area of spray opened into a keyhole and her key glowed blue. Chauncy followed, the brightness of the garnet's glow making the flames seem to writhe. When he'd backed away, I knew it was my turn. I stepped up to the door and watched as the key sparkled under my shirt with a soft yellow light. Removing the key from around my neck I followed their moves and watched in awe as the swirls moved like gears in a machine. They revealed my own keyhole. I inserted the key, and with one last look over my shoulder, turned it.

I stepped away and listed as a series of mechanisms seemed to click behind the door. One by one, Alexandar, Valerie and Chauncy walked forward again to touch their keys. I took the steps needed and touched mine as well.

"Think about your loft and specifically the doorway you want to walk through," Alexandar instructed. "Then turn the knob."

I did as he asked. I thought of my loft and how dirty I'd left it. I tried to picture my front door, but at the last minute thought of my closet. The compass seemed to vibrate. The keys released from their locks as the doorway morphed. I put mine back around my neck and watched as the door changed into any ordinary entrance. It now had a knob that I immediately took in hand and turned. It swung open to reveal a messy bedroom.

We shuffled into the room and the door closed behind us. It looked like a tornado had been through the place, beyond my normal messiness. Everything was torn apart, even my mattress was ripped. Stuffing hung out like it had been eviscerated. The pictures and paintings that were still lucky enough to be on the wall hung drunkenly.

"What happened here?" I asked.

"There's no telling," Chauncy walked to a wall and attempted to straighten a picture. The string on the back snapped and it crashed to the floor.

"Probably Agents trying to find any clue as to where you were," Alexandar said. He moved down the stairs.

It was then that I realized we'd all come from my closet. I went back to open the door, but there was nothing but my clothes and shoes. The items inside were shredded and disorganized, but no magical doorway back to our labyrinth.

"How does this work?" I asked, opening and closing the door repeatedly. "How do we get back?"

"That's simple," Valerie said. "Go to any door with a lock and use your key. You will find yourself back at our Sanctuary."

"Even if I'm alone?" I asked, looking over my shoulder.

"Even if," Valerie nodded. "Only two Elementals are needed to get off the island. Though there are ways to get off on your own, they are not recommended."

"Hmm," I pondered this while we went downstairs.

Alexandar walked from the back of the town house and shook his head.

"It's clear," he said. "Do you notice anything missing?"

"It would be hard to tell," I frowned as I looked around the destruction of what used to be my home. I walked to the front door and sifted through the pile of mail sitting under the slot.

"It looks like whoever tossed the apartment did so almost immediately after you took me," I said.

"Why do you say that?" Chauncy asked.

"The pile of mail here is almost undisturbed," I replied. "It looked similar to this when I came home from a lecturing circuit I was on a few months ago."

Sifting through the mail I saw one letter addressed to me from my brother-in-law. I opened it up and my eyes widened at the date. It had been over a week since I left. How was that possible? I looked up from reading.

"Does time work differently on the island?" I asked.

"Yes," Alexandar nodded. "Though just a bit slower. We think it has to do with being in the stratosphere."

"According to this I've been gone for over a week," I said.

Alexandar nodded.

"What else does it say?" Valerie asked.

I went back to reading it.

"My brother-in-law apologizes for the way he treated me the day that Samantha died," I frowned. "And that the boys need me. He says he's been by several times to the house and my work but no one had seen me so and he's getting worried. The funeral..."

I trailed off and looked at a calendar I'd nailed to the wall, that nail was probably the only reason it was still there. A clock lay broken and still working on the ground.

"I missed the funeral," I choked on the words. "They will be heading home soon."

I'd left my credit card on file for their hotel so that they could stay indefinitely near the hospital. It must have been easier to just stay there rather than go home. A thought occurred to me and I rushed around looking.

"Where is it?" I mumbled to myself.

"What are you looking for?" Valerie asked. "Maybe we can help."

"I'm looking for my address book," I said. "I kept it near the front door. Where is it?"

They spread out to help me look but it was nowhere to be found.

"We need to hurry," I thought of the monsters that had tried to hurt me. "We have to get to their house. They know where my family lives."

I grabbed my wallet from the pile of my things near the door and rushed outside. I whistled as soon as I got to the curb to hail a taxi. One pulled over right away and we piled in. I gave the address and the taxi sped off, only to stop a block later in the famous New York traffic. I tried not to bounce in my seat but this speed was not working for me.

"Can we go any faster?" I asked the driver. A harsh wind began to blow outside and batter the windows.

"Tabs," Alexandar turned from his position in the front seat next to the driver. "Calm down. We will get there as soon as possible."

"But I can run faster than this," I said.

"That might be true," he said calmly. "But are you going to run all the way to New Jersey?"

A storm began to brew outside. Behind the driver, I struggled with my emotions and looked out the window. I stared at the clouds as they were forming in the sky. They looked dangerous, dark and heavy with rain that threatened to spill over. I looked over to Valerie and she gave me a reassuring look. She was upset as well but she was doing a better job of keeping a lid on it. Thunder and lightning cracked nearby. Chauncy laid an encouraging hand on my leg. Almost as if my prayers were answered the traffic began to thin and we didn't have trouble for the rest of the trip. I watched the sky as we drove to my sister's little house near the shore.

It was a tiny little neighborhood where everyone knew each other. A taxi stuck out like a sore thumb in an area like this, where every neighbor wanted to know who was coming and who was going. I stopped the taxi a block away from my sister's house and we all piled out. Thunder rumbled again just above us. As we walked, I realized it was probably a good thing we'd let out a block away, the streets were full of cars. There was barely enough room for one car to go down the street unopposed, much less a taxi releasing its passengers. I watched as people, dressed in black and mourning veils, approached my sister's house.

"They're hosting a wake," I said thwacking myself in the forehead. "Of course they are."

It was tradition. Even if my brother-in-law hadn't wanted to throw a wake, my mother would have forced his hand. Not that the neighbors would have let him get away without one. The women in the area would have formed an unbreakable flood, dropping off food and all sorts of things for him. Then they would probably be trying to gauge when they could try and take her place. My hands began to shake at the thoughts.

"Hey," Alexandar grabbed my hand, halting my march toward the house. "What's up?"

"All they want is a show," I gestured toward the line of people making their way into the tiny home. "Those people didn't even know her, why do they care?"

Alexandar took my face gently in his hands and ran his thumbs over my cheeks, brushing away tears. I hadn't even known I was crying. He closed his eyes and slowly lay his forehead against mine. One of his hands moved to the nape of my neck and our breathing mixed.

"I understand," he said. "But you need to take a breath. You need to be strong for your nephews. We know at this point they are safe. If they weren't there no one would be going in and out like this."

I took a deep breath and tried to calm my frayed patience. His eyes opened and I stared into them. I thought about the boys and their lack of understanding about death. Their need for pizza. I wondered if there was pizza inside and made a mental note to order some if there wasn't.

"Ok," I swallowed and finished wiping my eyes. "I can do this."

"Good," he lifted his face from mine and an odd looked crossed his face. "There's something I need to tell you before we face the Agents, if they are in fact here today."

"What?" I prompted.

Alexandar looked back and forth between Valerie and Chauncy. They seemed to nod subtly. It made me nervous.

"What don't I know?" I asked.

I watched him open his mouth to answer but a screech cut him off.

"How DARE YOU?" A woman screamed as she came trudging down the sidewalk.

My mother. I watched with a detached sense of awe as she stomped toward me. How had I ever feared this woman? Her face was beet red with anger. What could she do to me that hadn't already been done at this point?

"How dare I what, mother?" I asked, suddenly exhausted.

"How dare you show your face around here after what you did?" She continued her stomping until she was right in my face. Her short stature had her up on her toes trying to get closer to intimidate me. Normally I would have shrank away but this time I didn't. I studied her curiously as she gestured emphatically with her words. Feeling like I was really seeing her for the first time.

"What did I do?" I asked.

"You made us pay for your sister's funeral by ourselves," she huffed. "You know your father and I can't afford that. We had to make some cuts and put a *budget* on her memorial. We couldn't even get a caterer for this poor excuse of a wake."

"She didn't want an over the top funeral, mother," I sighed.

"That's beside the point," her face turned a deeper red. "You had no right to disappear and take all your fancy money with you. How do you think your brother-in-law felt? Though maybe it was a good thing that you left. I know you've having sex with him. How long had that been going on? Did you even wait until she died to start that?"

My face must have registered some sort of reaction that she interpreted as shame, because she smiled deeply as my mouth just dropped open. What I was feeling had nothing to do with shame but a deep sense of disappointment and pity. This woman, whom I called mother, was deliberately trying to ostracize her only living daughter. I shook my head. I was tired of her awful attitude and cruelty.

"Didn't think I knew about that did you?" She crowed triumphantly. "Well your little display at the hospital was enough for me to understand where your loyalties lie, which is nowhere."

"Mother, this is neither the time nor the place for your wild accusations," I looked around and saw that a small crowd had formed at the front of the house. Curtains in the houses around us rustled.

"You afraid your new boyfriend will find out about your indiscretions?" She sniffed as she looked Alexandar up and down.

"I will never know what people see in you," she said.

"Enough!" Startled, I looked around before I realized that had come from me.

My mother seemed shocked as well but recovered quickly. I cut her off before she could say anything.

"You do not get to talk to me that way," I told her. Out of the corner of my eye I noticed the small crowd parting. "You do not demand money and then attempt to disparage my character."

Alexandar, Valerie and Chauncy moved next to me. A silent wall of support.

"You don't even know me," I spat.

"I know you," her eyes went to slits. "I know you were dropped on my doorstep in an ugly little basket. Ugly basket for an ugly baby."

The words that were about to spill from my mouth dried at the source.

"Didn't know that did you?" She smiled again. "Of course not. Because for all your education, you're still stupid."

"I..." The blood drained from my face as she chuckled.

"Evelyn," a soft voice came from behind my mother.

She turned and instantly went rigid. Then she seemed to collapse in on herself and began sobbing. My father, or the man I thought was my father, stood there.

"Oh, Thomas," she walked the couple feet between them quickly. "I'm sorry, I know we agreed to never tell her. She just pushes me, you know how she pushes me."

"I'll be taking her home now," he looked up from the sobbing woman who was currently soaking his shirt. "I apologize for any extra grief she caused you today. This is for you."

This was the most I felt I'd ever seen him speak. I was in awe. I'd almost forgotten what his voice sounded like when it wasn't thick and slurred. I took the envelope he offered without hesitation and stuffed it into my pocket.

He smiled at me through watery eyes and turned with his wife. I had always thought this man was my father, was it possible he wasn't? Together they walked up the street and disappeared.

The small crowd waiting by my sister's house began to disperse. I took a deep breath and my friends smiled at me encouragingly.

"Are you ready for this?" Alexandar asked. Still holding my hand he ran his thumb over the back.

"It can't be as bad as this was," I huffed out a broken laugh.

Turning hand in hand with Alexandar, we moved toward the house.

"Who are my parents?" I wondered as we walked into the front yard.

"That's a question we will attempt to answer after we ensure the safety of your family," Alexandar squeezed my hand.

I had a hard time forming thoughts. My entire world had just been turned upside down. We walked into an open room of hushed conversations, some of which halted at my appearance. I could only surmise that they were probably talking about me and what had just happened outside. The downstairs of the house was an open circle: to the left was the sunken living room, to the right was the sitting room. I walked to the left and through the living room, into the kitchen. The pocket door was open so that I could see the dining room table full of food. It was at the little breakfast nook where I found the three of them. Twin cries of joy escaped the boys, who wiggled out from behind the table and through the crowd of people.

I let go of Alexandar's hand to crouch down and intercept them.

"You came! You came!" Thomas yelled. He'd been named after the man I'd called father.

"Auntie Tabbie! Auntie Tabbie!" Tad threw himself into my arms while Thomas squeezed my neck.

"I'm sorry I'm late boys," their tears wet my shirt and neck.

"It's ok," Thomas whispered in my ear. "Because you're not dead."

"We were scared that you went to sleep and didn't wake up like mommy," Tad said a bit louder than Thomas had.

"Oh, Tabbie," Jon walked from the table. The boys let go so their father could have his turn. Jon hugged me close and I returned the embrace for his comfort. He held it a bit longer than I would have liked but pulled away as soon as I thought it was going on too long.

"We were so worried about you," Jon said.

Though he'd pulled away, he kept his hands on my shoulders and massaged them. I looked over at Alexandar who was frowning at us. I wanted to shrug off the hands, they were making my skin crawl. I didn't want to cause a scene so I took his hands and held them with mine, bringing them in front of me. Their coldness startled me. I looked at our joined hands, frowning.

"How can I help?" I asked.

"Make them leave," Jon leaned in close, his icy breath made my skin itch.

"Everyone?" I asked.

Jon nodded.

"Ok," I turned to the crowd at large and saw that many people were taking note of how close we were. Jon stepped up behind me put his hands on my hips. I moved away before he could lean in. I went to my friends, who were respectfully keeping their distance for our reunion. Alexandar wouldn't look at me. A pit began forming in the bottom of my stomach. I had some explaining to do. I wasn't sure how I would since I didn't know what was going on with Jon. He was probably just overcome by grief and needed someone familiar to hold onto.

"Can you guys help me clear the room?" I asked them. "Jon wants everyone out. He's done with the day."

"Sure," Valerie touched my shoulder as she moved past.

Chauncy smiled and nodded encouragingly. Alexandar just walked by without making eye contact with me. The pit in my stomach twisted and I sighed. We made our way through the rooms and when everyone was gone we sat down to watch the boys play in the living room.

"Tabbie," Jon said from the hallway. "Can I speak with you upstairs?"

"Of course," I stood from the chair I'd occupied, smiled at my friends and followed him upstairs.

He turned into his bedroom and faced the window so that when I entered the room I could only see his back.

"What is it, Jon," I asked.

"Close the door," he said.

I complied. Turning, I closed the door with a click, thinking that maybe he didn't want his kids to hear something. As soon as the door closed he was right behind me, hands on my hips pulling me back against him.

"Stop," I said and pushed away from him. "Jon, don't."

"You don't know how much I've wanted you," Jon groaned as I struggled. "You have no idea, do you?"

His tongue licked the side of my neck making me nauseous.

"Jon," I said after I managed to get some distance. "What are you doing?"

"I want you," he moved in and pulled me against him. "When I saw you with that person downstairs I realized just how much."

One of his hands snuck under my shirt to the bare skin underneath. A sharp pain had me pulling back.

"Ow," I pushed him hard enough that we switched positions, which I instantly realized was the wrong move. Now he was blocking the exit.

His smile seemed to split his face and his teeth gleamed brightly. I'd never seen him like this before.

"What is wrong with you?" I asked him, shaking my head. "Your kids are right downstairs."

"I don't care about them," brushing his hands through the air like they were nothing. "Leaches. Sucking the life out of me, of your sister."

"Jon," I started backing away as he came toward me again. "This isn't you."

I backed into a doorway and fumbled behind me for the knob. When it opened I quickly jumped inside and closed the door. I thanked all the powers above that my sister had wanted to transform one of their bedrooms into a huge walk in closet with a lock on the door. Jon pounded against it and I wondered how long the lock would last. The pounding stopped for a moment and in its place I heard a sickening growl. I shuddered and looked for an exit. I went to pull out my cell phone and realized I hadn't carried one since this weird journey began. Swearing, I began moving clothes around, looking for anything that I could use as a weapon. I opened a long mirrored panel door and something fell against me hard enough that I fell to the ground with a thunk. I rolled out from under it and stared down in horror.

It was Jon. His eyes were open and held an odd sheen to them, like he'd been held underwater. His head rolled oddly making my stomach roll. The throat was wide open and all I could manage to think was where the blood had gone. I knew how much blood there was in a human body but there was not a speck on his clothes. Nothing. What could have done this to him?

I remembered then, about the thing that had pretended to be my sister. Another bang at the door, louder this time. The lock began to give under the barrage. A rage took hold of me. This thing had killed my family. I let out a growl of my own. I stood and felt the air around me stir in response. I would never have used my element against my brother-in-law, but I would destroy the thing that killed him. I heard a crack of thunder, saw a flash from under the door, and the rain on the roof began to pound. The thing on the other side of the door howled in anticipation.

 Red. It covered my vision, flooded the room and changed the pretty things my sister had collected over the years into something sinister. I wanted to tear this thing apart. It had deprived me of yet another good person in my life. There were so few that losing two in the last few weeks was unacceptable. This was a loss I felt keenly. My chest tightened and my face hardened. I reached for the door and instead of opening it exploded into the bedroom. Splinters circled the room. Shrapnel embedded itself in the thing's arms, chest and legs. It howled. The explosion had knocked the creature back. As I entered the room it stood. Clothing sloughed off like a second skin. Its face had pulled back, revealing the sharks teeth I had known were there. The rage I felt was all consuming. In that moment it had the audacity to smile, though the term was loosely based around the fact it showed its entire set of shiny, dagger like, shark's teeth. Smile was a relative term.

I heard a pounding on the bedroom door but ignored it. Focusing on my rage, I threw a wall of air against the creature, pinning it to the wall. I watched as a large crack made its way up the wall and over the ceiling. The pounding got louder, accompanied by some muffled yelling. With an odd sense of detachment I saw the splinters around me, dancing in the swirls of air. A thought occurred to me and the pieces started hopping jauntily toward their target. It struggled against the wall.

"Tabbie," it cried in my sister's voice. "Tabbie please."

The splinters halted for a moment. This was just long enough for the beast to escape from my wall of air. The door burst open behind me, letting Chauncy and Alexandar step through. Chauncy had the same glowing orbs surrounding him from when I first met him, and Alexandar was crouched into a fighting stance. While I was distracted from the anger that had raged through me, the adrenaline that had been fueling the hatred began to abate and exhaustion took hold. I fought to keep my eyes open. I fell back into line with my comrades.

A sigh came from the window directly behind the beast. I watched as it stepped to the side and revealed a man sitting in the window, as if he were relaxing, enjoying a late summer breeze. He was unaffected by the near hurricane conditions that currently raged outside. Now that my vision had cleared I looked at the destruction of the room. Pieces of the frame and door were strewn about, leaving ugly destruction in their wake. A crack broke the room nearly in half, and water was beginning to leak through the roof.

The man let out a long suffering sigh again as I surveyed the room. He wore black leather, head to toe. His hair stuck out in unruly tufts and ended just above his shoulders. It looked like he'd failed to run a brush through it in years.

"It's beautiful, isn't it?" He asked. "The wanton destruction of property. The absolute best element in my opinion. Endless possibilities, unlike fire, earth, and water. You have boundless energy when you figure out how to influence it within its boundaries. But you haven't gotten there yet. A pity, though I didn't expect you to fill her shoes so quickly."

I just stared at him. He smiled in response to my study, but it was a flexing of facial muscles at best. There was no light in his eyes. It just seemed like something pale inhabited his body in comparison to true life. Everything about him seemed dull. The monotone he used, the way he sighed as if trying to laugh. It was disconcerting.

"Recognize him don't you?" He asked. "Of course you do, he's unforgettable."

He seemed to preen as it finally sunk in. The Doppelganger shifted and became the shark-toothed man who had pushed me into traffic. This man tried to take my choice from me. He tried to kill me.

"Where is she, Max?" Alexandar's voice broke my haze, crackling with suppressed anger.

"She's around," he shrugged as if annoyed anyone would want to talk to someone else.

A thought occurred to me.

"You're right," I said. "I do remember him."

This smile almost reached his eyes, but it looked more like the lighting on a corpse rather than a genuine smile from a living person.

"He used to deliver my pizza right?"

His face fell in a near comical fashion. I watched Chauncy shake with silent delight out of the corner of my eye.

"It's not smart to provoke me," he grumbled like a tired two year old.

Chauncy and Alexandar, by some silent signal, attacked simultaneously. Alexandar pulled his hands up and I watched in awe as vines attached to the man's feet. A ball of fire flew at his face and he took it point blank. During this attack Alexandar and Chauncy were closing in on him. With a flick of his hand they both flew backward. He tore his feet from the vines and wiped the singed area from his chest.

"I understand her," he scoffed. "But you two should know by now that your parlor tricks do nothing. I'm surprised you tried."

He waved another hand and we all fell to the floor. It felt as if a major weight was pushing us down. Gravity had intensified around us and I could barely move. Alexandar was stuck staring in my direction. It seemed as though a thousand conversations passed between us in the short amount of time.

I'm Sorry, he mouthed. I wasn't sure why he was apologizing. If he had done his best, there was nothing to apologize for.

"I was hoping your fourth friend would join us so I could take all of you out at the same time," Max yawned. "But it doesn't look like she's coming to your rescue. Might as well finish this now then."

Before it had been extremely difficult to breathe, now it suddenly became unbearable. I was unable to draw in air. My lungs compressed and I struggled, air slowly filling my lungs at my insistence. Seeing that Chauncy and Alexandar were having no such luck. Before I could attempt to fill their lungs I heard a loud crack before the floor gave way. It was enough to have each of us on our feet again within the moment of the distraction. Alexandar grabbed me and we dove behind a couch.

"How?" I breathed deep, the free air around me.

"We weakened the floor with our attacks," he responded, looking over the back of the couch. "He was right about the effect of our Elements on him when he's prepared for it. We need to catch him unawares."

"Well," the man sighed again, directly above the couch. "I figured it would take you longer to figure out that one."

I heard the snapping of jaws and whispering.

Alexandar and I rolled in opposite directions and ran.

"You are correct," the said to I would assume, the beast. "It may be time for a more physical application. You are approved to proceed."

I felt the ground shudder as the beast came up behind me while I ran.

"Which one?" It hissed. "Hmm, well I already know you taste absolutely divine. Yours is the blood I want first."

I was knocked to the ground and dragged through debris. I closed my eyes and breathed deep trying to keep myself from begging for my life. Everything was quiet for a moment and I felt a light breeze. The push against my body seemed to disappear. When I opened my eyes there was a sword next to my hand. I had no idea where it came from, or why. I looked up and realized that the beast was no longer moving. It was frozen, as was the man, who hovered nearby, watching in what I could only assume was reserved delight.

"How did you?" the man seemed incredibly confused when he began moving again, but he wasn't looking at me. He was looking down the hallway.

I moved quickly as the Doppelganger went in for the kill and without a second thought ran the blade into the monster's body. As soon as the blade entered its body it screamed. I looked behind me, to where the man had been looking, but there was no one. I pulled the sword, from the beast and it began to shudder.

"Why Tabbie?" It repeated in my sister's voice.

"You're not my sister," I said.

I watched in awe as the beast seemed to collapse in on itself. It folded into odd shapes and fell into the hole I had created inside its body, reminding me of flesh and blood circling a drain. Finally it disappeared with a sickening pop.

I looked for my friends, who had been coming to my aid and seemed just as confused as I was. The man let out a screech and I was flung against the wall. The sword clattered to the floor nearby. He held out his hand like he was using the force, and I couldn't help but laugh at the image.

"You think this is funny?" He asked. "Who are you?"

I frowned. At the moment, I didn't have an answer.

"I take life as if it's nothing," he demanded. "Who are you to challenge me? Perhaps I should take out your friends to get you talking."

He turned toward Alexandar and I struggled against the wall. "How do you know the Time Warden?" He demanded.

When I just shook my head he used his other hand and had Alexandar slam against the ceiling viciously. Tears clouded my vision at the realization that even with these newfound powers I was still helpless.

"Who are you?" Max repeated.

Walking over, he picked up the sword and held it at my throat.

"Fine," he said. "Since his life means so little to you perhaps I should end it."

"I don't know what you're asking," I cried, still struggling against the wall.

"Of course you do," he said.

I looked at Alexandar, who looked back at me. This time it was my turn to mouth, *I'm Sorry*.

Just as Max was about to touch the sword, he was knocked away. The sword was thrown back toward me, where it slammed into the wall. We were all released from the gravity well I slumped down the wall. Exhaustion gripped me. I felt drained. I looked to where Max had been thrown and a woman now stood on top of him while he struggled.

Her hair hung ruler straight and framed her face. It was jet black, just like her clothes.

"Causing problems again Maxine?" She chortled. "Can't you even take care of the newest Guardian?"

"There's something different about her," he gasped as she stood on his neck.

"Of course there is," she tsked. "There always is. But you've failed for the last time. I've got orders to take you out. I'm the leader now."

I watched in horror as she stomped on his neck, then created a vacuum around him, which tore his body to pieces in seconds.

"Moira," Alexandar's voice broke into my horror. Had he just called out for his sister?

"Oh, Alex," she smiled, but the same lack of emotion stole any warmth that may have been in the gesture. "I'm forever saving your ass, aren't I?"

"Moira," Alexandar trembled. "Please."

"Moira, please," she repeated mockingly in a whiny, nasally voice. "What? Please what? Please don't kill you? Please don't kill all of you?"

She sighed.

"I'm going to give you all a warning," she examined her nails. "I'm in charge of the Guardians of Chaos now, so you should be wary. I'm looking forward to the games we'll play."

"Why are you doing this?" Alexandar pleaded.

"Because I've seen the light," she answered succinctly. "And I need to enlighten you. Now you should all run before I change my mind and decide today is your day of reckoning."

Chauncy grabbed Alexandar by the shoulders, pulling him forcibly down the hall and out the front door.

"Oh and Tabitha?" Moira called after me when I picked up the sword. "You could never fill my shoes."

Turning, I ran after Alexandar and Chauncy. Alexandar was struggling lightly with Chauncy outside until he saw me exit the house, then we did as she suggested and ran.

"Where are the boys?" I asked Chauncy as we ran.

"Safe," he said.

We had to run a good distance before we found a taxi. Chauncy hailed it and we piled in, he gave an address and began moving.

"Why didn't our powers work on them?" I asked.

"The Elements can't function within the Void so if an Agent is aware it is easy enough for them to·deflect our attacks," Chauncy confessed. "How did you get that sword?"

"I have no idea, it just appeared," I told him truthfully.

"How do you guys normally fight them?" I wondered. "How do you normally fight them?"

"Blind luck and surprise attacks," Alexandar said bitterly. "Air has been a large contributor to the ones we've defeated. Mostly because it's kept us alive rather than actually doing any damage."

"Most times we usually meet them outside city limits where we can tear apart the terrain to fight them," Chauncy told me. "But that obviously wasn't an option today. One earthquake, one tornado, one fire or one flood and half the neighborhood would have been lost."

"So we risked a lot to save my nephews," I concluded.

"Yes," Chauncy nodded.

"They have no fear," Alexandar said.

This time Alexandar was sitting in the back with me and squeezed my hand. I was too tired to pull away like I wanted. It was taking all my energy to stay awake.

"Why did she call herself a Guardian of Chaos?" I yawned. It was becoming increasingly difficult to keep my eyes open. I leaned my head on Alexandar's shoulder since it was there and unoccupied, not because I wanted to be close to him.

"The Agents like to think of themselves as Guardians," his voice seemed far away.

"That seems oxymoronic," I said and gained a chuckle in response.

"Go ahead and sleep for a bit," Alexandar said.

But I was way ahead of him.

I woke to someone shaking me. I popped an eye open and saw Tad sitting cross-legged in front of me. The low fire in my bedroom hearth warmed the room and emitted a low light. I looked to the side and found Thomas sleeping next to me, curled into my back. Tad scooted closer and whispered in my ear.

"I just wanted to make sure you were still here."

Then he turned around and crawled under the blankets, scooting backward to snuggle up to me. I closed my eyes and did my best to steady my breathing. These two had been through so much in the last few weeks. First losing their mother, and now their father. I had a vague recollection of picking them up at some game center. Valerie had taken them away from the house and watched over them while we fought. This was all relayed to me while I was near dead on my feet. We had located the boys and Valerie at a nearby arcade. In order to make the trip back to the Sanctuary we had decided to find a less occupied area to use our keys so we piled back into the taxi to find a safer location. Immediately upon entering the cab, the boys took occupation of my lap. Tad had asked where their father was, but Thomas had just looked at me.

"He's dead too," he'd stated. It hadn't even been a question. I'd just nodded, holding back tears.

Tad made conversation with everyone and wondered when he would see his father again. How did you explain this to a child? No one should have to. We took them home with us so that I could figure out what to do. I couldn't subject them to being raised by my mother, and while my father may have cleaned up his act, I wasn't sure it could last. I was proud that I had been the catalyst in his change and I did forgive him. I knew it was a disease, but it was a disease without a cure. One had to be vigilant in their efforts to contain it. If not, one slip and it was back to square one. There was no telling what the damage would be this time.

Even though they weren't my blood, they were the last of my family. I wasn't going to let them go. When they were old enough to understand I would take them for a visit. Until then, I was their only protection. That was it. I was their last line of defense. It was a terrifying prospect. I had to learn all I could before the next battle, and there would be a next battle. I would make sure of it. But the first thing was to ensure my nephew's safety.

Valerie had mentioned that there was a kind of safe house for children orphaned by the Void. We would take them there. It felt like I would be abandoning them, but Valerie said that I could visit them as much as I wanted. I opened my eyes again and listened to the boys breathing. Every so often, Thomas would reach out for me in his sleep, just to make sure I was still there. Tad woke every couple hours to make sure I was alive. My heart broke for them both.

My eyes fell on the letter that lay open on the desk across the room. Where did I come from? Who was I? Where were my parents now? I'd never thought about it because I thought I'd known. I'd had fantasies as a child that I'd been adopted and my real parents had been high powered physicists that didn't have time for offspring. I would have understood and wanted to follow in their footsteps. When I'd grown out of that fantasy and found art, I'd just wanted to get out of the house as quickly as possible.

I had received scholarships and grants, but school had been expensive. The letter that said I had a full ride hadn't been from the college. It had come the same day as the acceptance letter so I just assumed it was a partner company that took a special interest in my graduating early. When I graduated Valedictorian I received a letter from the same company that offered further schooling, if I was been interested. I would need to dig out those letters to see if there was any clues. The company: Herr Wolff's Warren for Wayward Wards I'd thought the alliteration cute at the time, but now it posed more questions. I wondered now if they had something to do with my adoption.

The letter currently on the desk, was an answer of a different sort. I closed my eyes and read the letter all over again in my mind. I'd read it so many times the paper had begun to fray at the edges, I knew every crease and wrinkle in the paper.

My Dear Daughter,

I never did right by you. Let me try to make up for my mistakes by telling you the truth you deserve.

I will always consider you my daughter. Your mother and I discussed keeping this a secret but I'm not sure I would be able to live with myself if I didn't. I hope to see you at your sister's funeral because I want to tell you. Not to hurt you, but to relieve you of our burden. I hope you will still visit us, even though I haven't seen much of you the last few years. I don't blame you.

I love your mother with everything I have, but she can be hard on you. For you to understand why, you need to know about the day you came into our lives. Your mother had been eight months pregnant with our son and she miscarried. It was one of the worst days of our lives. We'd found out that day that she would never be able to carry another child. It was the darkest day that I can remember. Your appearance on our doorstep had seemed like a cruel joke. For this truth I am sorry. I know better than to blame a child for my problems, but I did. I couldn't forgive myself so I drank. I drank so much that I forgot what day it was or how old you were.

There had been a letter attached to your bassinet. It had read two simple lines: "This is Tabitha. While she lives with you, your bills will be paid."

The adoption paperwork had been in a diaper bag. It was all filled out, but the adoptive parents were closed to us. The only information about them had been a medical history, which didn't have anything in it except heart disease. All we had to do was file it. So that's we did. The checks began the day after we filed and came every other week until the day you left our house.

I thank you every day for asking me to sign your petition for emancipation. It woke me up. My daughter, attending an Ivy League college. The pride I felt, even under the booze, had been overwhelming. I had to ask myself, what was I doing with my life? You are the reason I could get out of that chair that I had been stuck to for too many years to count. You are my saving grace. I hope in your heart you can find the compassion to forgive my absence in your life.

Today I have been five years sober and I thank you every single day. You are the higher power I pray to, to help strengthen me during my dark moments. Your determination and perseverance are my model. Come visit soon.

Love,
Dad

I still didn't know how to process the confessions contained in the letter. That I could be the reason my father bettered himself was flattering, but what happens when he doesn't see me or if I go missing? Will he slip? He drank through my entire childhood. I could easily forgive him, but the truth is that I'd never hated him for his absence. I'd just never understood it. In a way, he was part of the reason I studied so much. I was terrified to end up like him, wasting away in front of the television. It seemed like a slow death that I would never be able to survive, like some terminal cancer. I needed to learn new things constantly. If I wasn't learning, it was almost as if I could feel my brain cells dying.

I concentrated on my breathing and tried to match it to the breathing of the small life forms surrounding me. They seemed so peaceful right now. I needed sleep, but I needed someone to hold me more than that. As I breathed deeply, I saw the beach from my first training session and brought it into focus around me. I felt the heat of the sand beneath my body as I stretched and the tickling breeze as it fluttered the branches above me. Two boys slept soundly on a blanket nearby. They seemed even more relaxed now that they were sleeping deeply under the dappled sunlight created by the shading trees. I listened to the breeze for a time before standing and walking to the nearby water. I let the water flirt with my toes and suck my feet deeper into the sand. The sensation was pleasant but reminded me uncomfortably of the nightmare I'd had my first night. Taking two steps backward, I sat in the sand and brought my knees up so I could rest my chin on them. The loneliness began to creep in and I wished for someone to share this time with. When footsteps fell behind me, and someone sat down next to me, I smiled. My smile quickly disappeared when I realized that it wasn't Alexandar.

"Who are you?" I asked.

"A friend," he replied.

He seemed out of place on the beach in his stark white three piece suit and black bow tie. His shoes were shiny and black, despite the small white sand crystals that clung to the sides. He held a black cane with a silver dandelion puff at the head, which he gently tapped against his shoes.

"Where's Alexandar?" I asked.
Something told me I could trust him, but I couldn't put my finger on why.

"He's asleep, as you should be," he replied.

"Why aren't I?"

"Because of this," he tapped his cane to his temple. "You've never been good at turning this off."

"That's true," I nodded and poked my lower lip out, pouting.

I felt so much like a child in that moment. It felt good to stop thinking just for a little while and feel my youth.

"Have we met before?" I asked.

"Yes," he smiled at me.

Though he was facing me, I couldn't make out his features. I could see his clothes, his hands, and a black fedora on his head. But I couldn't see his face. It was like looking through a really dirty window at the sun. I couldn't look at him for very long because it hurt my head. I looked away before it gave me a headache and rubbed my temples. A sense of Deja Vu was forming, like a long forgotten dream that was breaking the surface of my memory.

"Have we met here before?" Everything seemed suddenly very silly.

"Exactly here," he told me.

"This is our place isn't it?" I asked. "Even though I've never been here in real life before."

"That's right," he nodded.

"Why can't I remember?" I frowned and played with my lower lip, which felt numb.

"Because you're not meant to remember me yet," he said. "But I remember you."

He touched my nose and I laughed, clapping my hands together. They seemed much smaller than they used to be. I felt like I'd just won the lottery. I looked over at the boys on the blanket and they seemed to be no more than babies as they slept. As I watched they seemed to grow into men, then back to children again.

"Will I get to meet you soon?" I wanted to know.

"Soon enough," he said standing again. "Be patient."

"Will I remember you this time?" I asked, following his departure with my eyes.

"Not this time," he said. "But soon. Now sleep."

So I did.

 Waking from a vision as soothing as my dream had been was difficult, but wake I did. The boys still slept beside me so I did my best not to wake them as I climbed out of bed. As nice as the dream had been it faded, as any dream does. What one minute ago it had felt extremely vivid, now seemed bland and unworthy of my attention.

My first thought upon waking had been to research something, but I couldn't quite put my finger on what it had been. I puttered around the room while the boys continued to sleep, trying to remember I felt it would be unwise to leave them alone so soon after yet another tragedy.

Chauncy had taken the sword to put in the weapons room. I think he really wanted to study it, as did I. Until the boys woke, I wouldn't have an opportunity. I sat in one of the chairs in my room near the hearth and soaked up the warmth while I leafed through one of my books on control. It had all types of suggestions for different personality and Element types. I tucked away the information for later use. Lost in my reading, eventually I felt a tug on my sleeve.

Both the boys sat on the floor watching me read. I wondered how long they'd been there.

"Good morning boys," I uncurled from my seat. "Would you like some breakfast?"

At their nods I stood and took their hands, trying to reinforce our connection. I wasn't sure how I would be able to let them go to an orphanage. Perhaps we could keep them on the island for a while.

I watched as the boys eyes popped wide at the assortment of food on the buffet table. I was more than a little surprised as well. Where normally there were fruit, eggs, toast and other normal breakfast fare, today there was an abundance of sweets. Cakes, cookies, doughnuts and all types of yummy looking food. There was even a chocolate fountain. I calculated in my head the cavity expenses but quickly shoved it aside when they both squealed in delight and ran for the table. Their plates were piled high within seconds and they both carefully walked to the table, so as not to drop a crumb.

Chauncy, Valerie and Alexandar were already there. I found a small warmer filled with eggs and toast to fuel myself and sat between the boys. Two tall chairs had been stuck on either side of my seat. The boys chatted endlessly with the others at the table while I picked at my food. It was a relief to see that they had forgotten their plight, at least for a little while. It gave me hope to see their resiliency. Before too long, they sank back into their quiet demeanor and began picking at their food as I was.

"You know boys," Alexandar cleared his throat. "I made a special request for this food to be made for you."

"That reminds me," I looked up. "Who cooks the food and tends the hearths? I've never seen anyone."

"Ah, well," Alexandar seemed delighted as if I'd just helped him with something. "That would be our faerie staff."

"Faeries?" The three of us said together.

"Why yes," Alexandar's grin spread and he looked at me. "You haven't seen them because you don't believe."

"Of course not," I scoffed and turned back to my food.

"I saw a little dancing flame add wood to the fire last night," Tad turned to me, eyes large.

"You did not," Thomas stuck his tongue out.

Tad's lower lip began to shake and it finally occurred to me what Alexandar was attempting to do. I sighed at my density when it came to children.

"You know," I forced a smile onto my face. "I think I saw that too."

Tad's eyes immediately dried and shone with a hint of worship.

"You did?" Though he had been skeptical of his little brother, Thomas was completely trusting of my opinion.

"Mhmm," I began to eat with earnest though I wasn't hungry.

"Wow," Thomas turned to his food and followed suit.

"Can we catch one?" Tad wanted to know.

"Hmm," Alexandar winked at me. "Well now, let me think. There are a few ways to catch faeries."

While I mentally cringed, I kept an outward air of excitement. It was like setting the boys up for Snipe Hunting. The few times I'd met my grandfather he'd attempted to get my sister and I engaged in similar quests. He had described the Snipe in great detail and told us how to catch it, only to laugh at our antics. I had caught on quickly and abandoned the hunt, but my sister had continued. I asked her later why she did and her answer had confused me, *"Because Grandpa was having so much fun watching us."*

Samantha had always been the first to think of another's feelings over her own, unlike myself. The boys needed selfless right now.

"Tell us more," I feigned enthusiasm. It seemed to be working, the boys leaned forward and were more engaged than I'd seen them since their mother was injured.

"Gather round," Alexandar gestured for the boys to come closer. "These tactics are a secret and cannot be shared with everyone."

"Go on," I smiled. "I have some research to do."

Clearing my plate, I watched as they ducked their heads in close to Alexandar and giggled. When Alexandar looked up and winked again my heart felt like it dropped to my feet while my stomach turned flips. He was so handsome despite his disheveled appearance. I smiled back at him and turned to the small kitchenette to place my plate in the sink. I noticed how clean everything was and glanced over my shoulder at the three of them huddled together. Frowning, I walked toward the library. There may be something to the faerie thing, it would explain why the staff was not seen nor heard. I decided to look it up in the library today.

The barren walls with ambient torch light had begun to feel like home. Though it looked like it should be dank, musty and closed in, there was an inexplicable breeze that made me feel like I was just about to walk through one of the doorways to the outside. I turned into the library and ran my hands over the intricate woodwork of the archway as I passed beneath it.

Faeries, I considered. Then tossed the idea away.

I looked at the enormous card catalog and shook my head. I was going to try something different. If a lot of books in this library were enchanted I may be able to just ask questions and have them answered, rather than seeking them out. I picked a random set of stacks and started walking. I always enjoyed walking while I researched. It usually ended with me walking into something because my nose had been stuck in a book. However, with the advent of audio books made it easier to glean knowledge while multitasking. This felt similar, only more surgical in its information aspect. Similar to a search of an internet engine, I could walk down a stack and ask a question. In some cases I would have multiple answers back, creating an interesting cacophony of voices.

It seemed odd that the books did not all have the same voice. They were all very unique, almost as if I were surrounded by a million people, all experts in their own field. The accessibility of information was intoxicating. It wasn't until I stumbled upon a well-used reading area that I realized I had wandered into a part of the library I had never been yet.

There were stacks of books and empty coffee mugs, stains on the carpet and notes everywhere. What was this place? As if in opposition, the wooden planks surrounding the little study nook sparkled in their cleanliness. It was a perfect circle of dirt and decay. Books were caked with dust as if they'd stood in the same place for over twenty years. I stepped into the circle and it felt like there was a collective sigh of relief from the floor boards.

Under the dirt, the table was long and made out of rich mahogany. There was only a single chair, high backed and regal in its loneliness. I pulled it out and the scraping seemed to echo through the stacks. I swear I heard the sound of wings rustling, like bats in an abandoned cave. It had a shiver running down my spine. I couldn't put my finger on it, but this study area seemed like it had been waiting for me.

"How did you get in there?"

Startled, I jumped back from the table. Alexandar was standing on the other side of the clean line. The only footprints through the dust were my own. He circled the dust to face me.

"What do you mean?" I frowned at him.

"I mean," he pounded on a barrier that apparently kept him from entering the circle.

An odd electricity crackled and split the barrier like blue ice, then healed itself almost instantly.

"Extraordinary," I reached through the barrier that I hadn't seen.

Nothing happened. I touched Alexandar and felt the electrical pulse around me. I pulled him forward but I couldn't pull him farther than the invisible barrier.

"So very interesting," I closed my eyes and felt with my hands for the barrier, but I couldn't feel anything. "Hmm."

My eyes popped open and saw Alexandar was still directly in front of me where I'd left him. His eyes were on mine and there was an odd glint to them, almost as if he were studying me. It was a look I likely had on my own face when confronted with a new problem. I wasn't sure why it made me feel uneasy.

"What?" I asked.

"Just wondering who you are," he shook his head.

"You know who I am," I raised a brow.

"I thought I did," he frowned. "But now I'm wondering again."

My stomach was doing back flips at his nearness and perusal. I took one step back and cleared my throat.

"Where are the boys?" I changed the subject.

"They are busy setting out saucers of milk and waiting for the faeries to take a break," he chuckled.

"That's good," I cocked my head. "You're very good with them. What does the barrier feel like?"

"Your mind seems to derail thoughts quickly," he moved as if to touch me, but pulled back when the barrier stood firm. "Pins, needles and a current of static electricity."

He pushed at his mop of hair, which did look to be standing on end.

"What element controls Electricity?" I asked.

"None of them exactly," he frowned and his eyes moved to the dirty table. "Except..."

"Except?" I repeated.

"Go over to the table and look through the notes," he directed. "I have a hunch you may find dandelions among them."

"You think it's the Time Elemental?" Something about that rang true for me.

"It's a hunch," he shrugged.

"It would make sense in a way," I rustled through some of the pages. "Quantum physics and the polarization of time are just in the infancy of experimentation. There is so much we don't know about time and how it works. This could just be a manifestation of the type of power the Time Elemental has."

There were near unintelligible scribblings across mountains of papers, some covered in coffee rings, some with other substances I didn't care to examine. I paused when I came to a stack of five leather volumes, numbered by roman numerals on the spine. The top one seemed the oldest, but what made me pause was the hand print in the thick dust that covered it. There was no layer of new dust on top of the handprint. I examined my hands to see if I had inadvertently touched the stack. Though my hands were dirty, they lacked the thick layer of grime that would have been evidence of touching the volumes.

"Did I touch this stack of books?" I looked over my shoulder at Alexandar.

"No," he stood on his tip toes, trying to see the table.

"There's a recent handprint on them," my brows furrowed.

"Be careful," he said. "It's unlikely a trap, but be cautious."

I nodded. I felt a powerful pull from these books and I was curious about what they contained. As I slowly reached toward the book an image popped into my: of a cane with a silver dandelion head. The vision made no sense, but it continued to solidify into a memory when I finally touched the soft leather volumes. The edges curled backward from repeated use and the ware was obvious. At the immediate time of contact I heard a loud and comfortable laugh. It seemed to echo inside my head, speaking of delight and joy.

"Did you hear that?" I asked Alexandar without taking my eyes off the book.

"Hear what?" He asked.

"The laughter," I smiled as the sounds faded and opened the cover.

"I think I knew him somehow," I said.

"Him?" Alexandar asked.

"Yeah," I gestured to the volumes. "Him. Look, I think I'm going to be a while here."

I looked over my shoulder again at Alexandar, who nodded.

"I will come back in a couple hours," he turned to leave and then called over his shoulder. "We can start your training when you're done."

I nodded absently, my vision remaining on the books in front of me. I picked up the one on top of the pile and opened it. The first page was covered in ink drawings of dandelions in different stages of life. The second page was a very old and stained looking journal log.

February 28, 1680

Suddenly I have found a need to write down my thoughts. My dreams are fraught with the life and death of dandelions. I know not why. It is an obsession that transpired soon after my near death experience. It was terrifying and exhilarating.

I witnessed as a child ran into the road from a sweet Shoppe without looking. A passing carriage had been racing through and I watched, horrified as it bared down on the small figure. Without thinking I dove for the child and knocked her out from under the hooves. I was nearly trampled myself, except something amazing happened. Time stopped.

It quite literally halted in its tracks. The Divine was looking out for me that fine day and now I feel that something big is about to happen. I am driven to record it for posterity. I must.

J.R.

I sat at the desk and stretched. My back felt sore from standing. It seemed odd that it would hurt so quickly.

"What does it say?" Alexandar must have returned quicker than he'd planned. He put his hands in his pockets.

"I think it's the journal of the Time Elemental," I stared at him owlishly. "But if this is correct that he must be almost four-hundred years old..."

"What?" Alexandar blinked at me. "Let me see that."

I stood and walked over to hand it to him. About halfway there it ripped itself out of my hands and landed right back on top of the pile.

"It's well protected," Alexandar frowned. "And it seems it's only meant for some who can enter this circle."

I looked at the stack of books and papers. I wanted nothing more than to sit and read all of it.

"I wish I could just dive in," I sighed as I walked out of the circle of clutter. "But I need to learn more about my own element before learning another."

It was almost painful leaving the table of knowledge behind but I needed to learn about my own control. I made a mental note of where the stacks were so that I would be able to easily find my way back. Alexandar took the lead and we ended up in an area that looked like a tiny classroom, complete with wooden flip top desk and black board. Already written on the board was "Elementals 101: Theory and Practice".

"Smart to phrase it like a class I would take," I chuckled.

"I set this up yesterday while you took care of the boys," he walked to the blackboard. "I knew that you would need something to work on."

"Let's get to work," I sat at the desk and lifted the lid to reveal notebooks, pens, pencils and highlighters in a multitude of colors.

Pulling out the supplies I needed, I closed the lid and set myself up for a long class session. I wasn't disappointed. The boys wandered in and out a few times throughout the day. They brought us snacks and excited news about their faerie adventures. I marked time by their arrivals and departures. When they'd left for the third time I stretched and marveled at the two notebooks I had filled. Alexandar was a fount of information.

"Let's call it a day," he stretched as well. "We will pick it up again tomorrow."

"Alright," I nodded and put my supplies back in the desk.

Tucking the notebooks I'd filled under my arm I stood and we began our trek out of the library.

"How did you learn all this?" I touched the journals.

"Years of research," he stated flatly. "It's come in handy."

"I appreciate it," I yawned. "Though I enjoy researching and meandering around on my own, I need a crash course if I'm to hold my own weight next time."

"I'd say you did well enough on your own," Alexandar said.

"If time hadn't stopped again," I shuddered. "I doubt it would have ended so well."

"Time stopped again?" Alexandar stopped and turned to me. "When?"

"Right about the time I would have died," I said. "That's when the sword appeared."

"Is that why he was screaming about how you did it?"

"I would assume so," I shrugged and continued on. "I need to find a way to attack the Agents of the Void if our Elements don't work on them."

"That sword seemed to work rather well," Alexandar's brow furrowed.

"Has Chauncy found anything out about it?"

"Only that it is extremely volatile. Anything it pierces seems to disappear into some sort of black hole," he said.

"Curious," I sighed as we exited the library. "So your sister..."

"Is an Agent of the Void," Alexandar frowned. "Yes."

I felt as if he'd been dreading this conversation. As would I, if the positions were reversed. Part of me felt like dropping the subject, but I was hurt that he hadn't told me. We'd been through a lot recently and I felt a little betrayed by his omission.

"Why didn't you tell me?" I asked.

"Because I hoped it wasn't true," he said.

"But Valerie and Chauncy, they knew," I stated.

"Yes," he said. "Because they were there."

"So you don't trust me," my frustration was evident.

"No," he stopped. "That's not it at all."

"Then what?" I tried to continue down the hall.

"I..." He grabbed my arm. "Can you just stop moving for one second?"

"No," I slipped out of his grip.

I knew I being irrational but his deception had hurt my feelings more than I wanted to admit. Especially to him.

Alexandar caught up to me easily and pushed me forcefully against the wall. He imprisoned my arms against the wall and I struggled against him. When I didn't break free easily, I turned my head away and stared off into the darkness of the corridor.

"What?" I gritted my teeth.

"You don't understand," his breathing was ragged.

"That's an understatement," I scoffed.

"I wanted you to trust me," he said.

I glanced at him and he seemed to be struggling with himself. My anger drained away and was replaced by a very intense pull. I closed my eyes and tried to fight it. This wasn't logical. Just moments ago I'd been in a near rage, and now I was struggling to not pull off his clothes and jump him where we stood. What was he doing to me?

"How am I supposed to trust you when you lied to me?" I wanted to know.

"I'm sorry," his voice was soft as a whisper and his grip lightened on my arms.

"I don't like feeling helpless," I said.

"Neither do I," his breath was on my neck.

"What do we do?" I asked.

"I can think of a few things," his lips brushed just under my jaw sending shocks across my skin.

I sucked in air and nearly choked on it. It was deliciously wicked the way he chuckled with his lips soft on my neck. I lifted my neck to give him better access and sighed when he kissed the exposed flesh.

"Aunt Tabbie?" A call from down the hall had us jumping away like a child caught in the cookie jar.

"Yes?" I cleared my throat as Tad appeared out of the darkness, excitement in every movement.

"We caught one!" He jumped up and down.

"Caught one what?" My eyes were still glued to Alexandar's. A heat seemed to radiate between us.

"A faerie!" He clapped and ran back the way he'd come.

"A faerie?" All thoughts of what we had just been doing fled as the improbability seeped in.

"A faerie," Alexandar nodded and followed Tad, beckoning me forward.

I sighed. I wasn't sure I was ready for faeries to be real.

The food had changed on the buffet table but it still held a variety of junk foods. When I walked into the dining room I half expected there to be a box held up by a twig, with a string that stretched to Thomas. What I found was even odder than that. It looked as if there was a small breeze shuffling salt and pepper around on the dining table.

When I looked at Alexandar he just chuckled and nodded. I didn't understand what was happening. The boys bounced excitedly in place as the condiments swirled around like someone was sifting through them.

"I don't get it," I frowned.

"You don't see them?" Thomas giggled.

I wasn't sure what I was supposed to be seeing so I stayed quiet.

"She doesn't believe," Tad tugged on his older brother's shirt.

"But she knows everything," Thomas whispered.

"Knowing is not believing," Alexandar strode forward and crouched to be on eye level with the table. "Hello my friends, cleaning a mess are you? Well we appreciate it."

"I thought you said you caught one?" I asked the boys.

"We did," Thomas began to pout. "But Alex said not to keep them, because they are *really* fragile and we could hurt them if we even touch them. Like butterflies."

"So we made a mess they had to clean up by themselves!" Tad cheered.

"I still don't understand," I crouched down next to Alexandar.

"The boys mixed pepper and salt together," Alexandar pointed at the black and white sand on the table. "Faeries dislike waste, you see. So instead of dumping it all in the garbage they are separating the tiny grains by hand and putting them away."

As I watched I saw the miniscule pieces separating. What I'd perceived as just swirling was actually sorting and sure enough, small amounts at a time were making their way back into the shakers.

"How..." I started.

For a moment I thought I saw the air around the salt and pepper piles shift, but then it was gone.

"There are an innumerable species of faerie," Alexandar smiled at me. "You will see when you believe."

"I've accepted my reality," I looked back at him. "So why can't I see them?"

"Accepting your reality is different than having faith or believing in something you can't see," Alexandar explained.

I turned around, half expecting to see things hanging from the rafters and dancing around. I saw nothing beyond the normal.

"Where are they?" I asked.

"They still make themselves scarce," Alexandar said. "Regardless if you believe or not they still don't enjoy our company. They serve the Elements and by proxy us. But they do not appreciate us considering them our servants. Which of course you are not."

Alexandar held up both hands in peace at the empty table. I frowned.

"Well," I smiled at the boys. "That was exciting wasn't it?"

"I can't wait to tell..." Thomas' face dropped like a stone, bringing him crashing back to reality. "Will I ever be able to go home?"

This was a discussion I had been hoping to avoid for a while yet.

"That's a good question Tom," I took his and Tad's hands leading them to the sitting area.

Alexandar was tactful enough, or perhaps scared enough, to beat a hasty retreat.

"You know how much stock I put into education," I started.

I paused when the boys seemed lost immediately into my rehearsed speech and decided I may need to readjust my phrasing.

"I know you don't think it's important now," I continued. "But it will be one day. I would like to keep you both with me here forever, but I'm afraid you would get too lonely without other children to play with. There is a school for special kids like you."

"I get to go to school?" Tad's eyes filled with delight.

"You're sending us away?" Thomas' eyes spilled over and he pleaded with me. "We can be good! I promise!"

Seeing his brother's reaction Tad picked up the theme and immediately began crying as well.

"Oh honey," I picked them both up and cuddled them in my lap. "I will visit as often as I can. But it's not safe for either of you."

"When do we have to leave?" Thomas sniffled.

"I was hoping you both would keep me company for a few days longer," I hugged them close. "But then we will need to find the school for you."

"Why can't we just go to school here, like you?" Thomas crossed his arms stubbornly.

"Because the things you learn here," I sighed. "They are not the formal education I would like you both to have. Valerie has told me about this school and it sounds like you get to learn as much as you want, as well as play with the other children who are like you."

Children who had been orphaned by the Void. I had wanted to tell them but I didn't think that it would have helped in this instance.

"So let's have as much fun as possible while you're here ok?" I hugged them again and they both nodded slowly.

The next several days passed quickly to my never ending regret. I did not sleep much during those days. I was exhausted but I wanted to spend every waking moment with the boys. When they were sleeping, I was learning. And I had learned so much in such a short time. The journals called to me, but I knew I needed to focus on the task at hand. Once I had mastered my Element, only then would I allow myself the pleasure of new exploration.

When the day finally came to take the boys to the orphanage I wasn't sure if I could do it. As much as I disliked the person who had called herself my mother, I couldn't help but wonder if their lives would be better. I knew the woman would dote on the boys and the man who had called himself my grandfather would take care of them all. When I said as much to Alexandar, he gave me a sad smile and dashed my hopes.

"They will never be safe, as long as you live," Alexandar told me.

I nodded and packed the very few things they treasured now. I saw no problem with the boys taking a couple of the children's books from the library and some loose things they had collected from their adventures in the sanctuary. We had even ventured above for a while so they could run through the forest on the island and get some sunshine. It had been a risk but the boys had needed it badly, and so had I. That day had been one of the best, but now their time here was done.

We all gathered in front of the door and held our keys. Alexandar took pointe and we all inserted our keys. It was just as exhilarating as the last time. I listened to the boys' indrawn breaths and exclamations. When Alexandar opened the door we all walked through. It was dark, but Chauncy hurriedly created his little suns and it warmed the area quickly. I touched the wall and realized it was pressed rock. It had a damp feel to it but it was smooth, like a tumbled stone.

"Down this way," Valerie walked to the right as the tunnel veered off in fifteen different directions. The boys followed quietly.

In fact we were all very quiet. It felt like a funeral procession. After what felt like a hundred twists and turns we finally came to a door. It was a large paneled double door with beautifully carved handles. Valerie knocked lightly and the doors opened wide by a butler in full uniform. He bowed to us all and put out his arm to welcome us into the foyer. I goggled at the interior.

An enormous crystal chandelier hung from thirty foot high ceilings. Two staircases wrapped upward to a second and third floor. Beautiful art, which reminded me of my previous employment, hung on the walls. A second set of double doors opened underneath the framing staircases to a ballroom the size of a football field.

In the middle of the room was a bust of a grumpy man's head with a plaque below it: *Herr Wolff's Warren for Wayward Wards.*

My mouth dropped open. This was the place who had funded my education?

"Welcome," a tall, slender woman, wearing the clothes of an old style schoolmarm, walked out of the ballroom. "We've been expecting you."

She crouched and held out a hand to the boys, who shook her hand in turn. I wanted to dive into questions about my background, but this may not be the best time. I needed to try to get this woman alone so she can answer my questions.

"My name is Miss Abigail Wolff," she smiled at the boys. "Who might you be?"

The boys clung to my leg and my stomach dropped to the floor. How could I leave them? "This is Thomas and Tad," I squeezed them close.

Miss Wolff seemed to sense my apprehension.

"Why don't you follow me," she stood and gestured. "And we will tour the compound."

I took a boy by each hand and we followed Miss Wolff into the ballroom while Alexandar, Chauncy and Valerie stayed behind.

"Through here is the main ballroom," she threw her hands wide to encompass the space.

Space seemed to be a relative term for the expanse of rich hardwoods and marble pillars. I'd had my share of state dinners and charity auctions but none could compare to this. Velvet curtains were pulled back from floor to ceiling paneled windows. They let in a surprising amount of light, given we were supposed to be far below ground.

"How far below ground are we?" I asked.

"If you're worried about our security, don't be," Miss Wolff continued walking as she spoke. "We only have a few entrances and exits and they are well secured. Now if your question stemmed from the light we have a number of UV lights set up in our garden area, which allows for a very realistic sun like experience."

Realistic sun like experience. What was I getting these boys into?

"The ballroom is used for supervised exercise," Miss Wolff continued. "We have a number of activities that rotate on given days of the week: fencing, gymnastics, and archery among them."

I looked down to gauge the boys' reaction to the activities and they didn't seem too thrilled.

"Through here are the dining halls and kitchen."

Miss Wolff opened a set of white paneled doors to reveal what looked like a high school cafeteria and an open kitchen behind a standard Plexiglas covered buffet table. Everything seemed well lit and sterile. Images of past high school persecutions played through my mind and made me shudder. I hoped the boys would not have to live the horrors I dealt with in school.

"There are three full meals served per day, but there is always something available in case the meal just isn't quite enough. We want the children to feel comfortable, as if they were with their loved ones."

I nodded when she looked back at me and smiled. I hoped the guilt wasn't too apparent in my expression.

"Where are all the other children?" I asked.

"Thankfully we do not house as many as we once did," Miss Wolff turned off into what looked like a common room with three separate televisions, couches and chairs pulled around them. A few scattered children sat around one television that was playing what looked like an episode of *Days of Our Lives*. Some looked over at our entry and others pretended not to notice.

"*Days of Our Lives* seems an odd choice for children," I commented.

"This is the school's weekend," Miss Wolff responded, smiling at the children around the television. "So the children have two days of free time or for some time to catch up on some homework. *Days of Our Lives* reminds many of the children of home, rather than the cartoons that many children watch. Some of these kids have grown up faster than you would hope."

With a cough and an embarrassed smile one of the kids hopped up and ran off while Miss Wolff chuckled.

"We are strict with lights out and what time classes are to be attended," she walked through yet another set of double doors. "But we do our best to accommodate every child's needs."

I began to wonder if this school was connected to the library somehow, it also seemed to go on forever.

"Down there is the art and music room," she pointed down the hall that passed under another set of stairs. "Up there is the dormitories, a through here is my office."

She pulled out a set of keys to unlock her tiny door. A key winked out at me from the ring that looked a lot like the Elemental keys before she put them in her pocket. I made a mental note to ask Valerie about that later.

Miss Wolff's office was the smallest room out of everything we'd seen so far. It looked like it should have been a janitor's closet.

"I appropriated the chemical store room as my office because the actual supplies needed a bigger room," she chuckled. "It gets a bit cozy in here, but we needed the space and it's all for the greater good."

The boys had death grips on my hands and before we could attempt to cram into the minute space a very quick staccato clicking came our way in the form of a puppy. The boys dropped my hands so quickly it was almost comical.

"Puppy!" They both squealed and pounced to the very real delight of the canine.

"Hennessy!" A harassed looking cook came barreling out of the common room door brandishing a soup ladle like a club. "I swear I will make you into soup the next time you jump on my table and steal my meat!"

The thickness of the man's French accent made his speech near impossible to understand.

"Jacques," Miss Wolff's tone chilled the air by about ten degrees.

"Abigail, I told you to keep that *thing* out of the kitchen," he puffed his chest and stuck the soup ladle conspicuously behind his back. "I will thank you to keep my area sanitary."

"Hmm," Miss Wolff arched a brow and I watched as the gears turned inside her head. "Well it seems I will need two helpers to keep tabs on Hennessy, won't I?"

"We can help!" Thomas volunteered immediately. Tad nodded so vigorously I was afraid he may hurt himself.

Miss Wolff made a shooing motion at the cook. The man bowed and scooted backward while cursing in French. I wasn't fluent but I did pick up a few words to the effect of snotty, spoiled and something about servitude. I shrugged it off and turned back to the boys, who were receiving very specific instructions.

"He eats twice a day," Miss Wolff was telling them, then she looked at me and lowered her voice. "And needs to go outside often. I will show you everything you need to know today but it's a secret. So we have to wait until your Aunt leaves."

The boys looked back at me and I had to hold firm. It took all my strength to smile, rather than burst into tears. The look of betrayal was gone, but I knew they didn't want me to go. I crouched down and hugged them both close.

"I will come next week to see how you two are doing," I told them. "It seems as though you are in great hands and Miss Wolff knows how to contact me if either of you needs anything. I love you both so much."

Tad was crying and begging me to stay. Thomas took his hand and pulled him close. It was a heartbreaking image and I thought fleetingly that Thomas' childhood was over. He was still so young, but he looked at me with dry eyes and nodded, as if to say he could handle it from here. How could he when I wasn't sure if I could? I kissed them both one last time and left them in the very capable hands of Miss Wolff. I needed to get out of there before I lost all composure.

My last vision was of Thomas holding Tad close, lip firmed and eyes shining. I knew it would haunt my dreams for the rest of my life. They had endured so much loss in such a short time and here I was, adding to it. My resolve wavered for just a moment, then I turned and left them. Their sobs echoed behind me. If the attack on myself was any indication of the safety of the island, then I knew there was no way I could keep the boys safe in the Sanctuary. This was unfortunately the only option. Perhaps when they were older... I let that thought die before it began. Who was to say that I would survive the next twenty four hours, let alone the next decade?

I stepped into a private alcove to compose myself. The boys' cries had followed me and were echoing down the hallway. I hated myself. A lump had formed in my throat and I had a difficult time swallowing. My chest felt heavy and my eyes burned. Taking a deep, shuddering breath I tried to fight off the tears. I leaned against the walled and banged my head backward, then let myself slide to the ground. I couldn't breathe. The hiccupping sobs wracked my body. I barely noticed when I was picked up off my feet and cradled in large arms. I curled in and let them hold me. It wasn't for some time that I realized it was Chauncy who held me.

I took another shuddering breath.

"Take your time honey," he brushed the hair from my sticky face. "Let yourself feel, the good and the bad. Don't push it down. It can fester if you do."

He held me close and the feeling of someone being there had tears streaming anew. No one had ever held me just like this before. Without reservations. Unconditional support. When my eyes had dried enough, I sat up and gave him a watery smile.

"Let's go," I said.

After we had returned to the sanctuary I went straight to the library to get lost. It didn't occur to me until too late that I had failed to ask the woman questions about my background and who the money had come from for my schooling.

It felt as though the walls were judging me. Though I still could not see them, now that I knew they were there I could feel the faeries. Though that also could have been my sleep deprived brain overreacting to the outside emotional stimuli as well. Any lore I'd ever read as a child said they preferred human children over adults, so more than likely they may be the silent judges I felt.

Without realizing it I'd made my way to the abandoned study area. It was just as I'd left it last and I entered the area without resistance. Immediately, I picked up the journal I'd set down to prioritize my training. I could take a day for myself. What better way to get lost than by reading about another's life. I sat in the dusty, uncomfortable chair and opened the journal.

March 1, 1680

I have lived this colonial life since I was born. My father had moved to the Americas from England after King Charles awarded him land in a new colony called Carolina. My mother came with him and had me soon after they landed. Together they built a new life and my father ran the ship yards, assuring only English ships were allowed to leave port with goods to trade. It is an honest life and one he expects me to assume.

But today is the day I leave. I have left a note and even now am sitting in a carriage that is taking me as far West as it will go. It is an untamed land I seek. I wish to make a life for myself, not to continue a life that was handed to me. My brother had always been more interested in the ships than I ever was.

There is a pull in this direction that I cannot deny. It calls to me more than any soft life I could have lead in this tiny colonial town. I wish to live.

J.R.

March 3, 1680

I had a dream last night during my travels. I dreamt of a field full of dandelions. They were in full bloom and stretched as far as the eye could see. A strong gust came through and blew their seeds into a beautiful whirlwind.

Today I found the exact field and watched as the seeds blew into a dust devil. A cold chill had crawled up my spine and squeezed my heart. What is happening to me?

J.R.

March 5, 1680

I have reached the farthest outpost and will now have to continue on my way. With the last of my money, I purchased a small covered wagon and a horse. The wagon is being loaded with food and supplies as I write. I will admit that I am nervous about the Indian inhabitants on the roads. From what I understand they will kill on sight. I have purchased a small pistol and blade for my protection. I wasn't entirely sure I would be able to use them, but the man had shown me how to load it and how to clean it.

I have months of travel in front of me. I only hope that I reach my destination safely. Where my destination is, I'm still not sure. I just know I have to go West. I will reach it and when I do, I will know it for my destiny.

J.R.

The rumbling in my stomach pulled me out of the pages that consumed me. I had to know more. I rubbed my gritty eyes and wondered how long I'd been here. When I sat up, my back cracked and my legs were pins and needles. Perhaps it was time to take a break.

I found a plate with a sandwich and chips, as well as a soda, on the floor outside the circle. Someone was looking out for me. I smiled and thought of Alexandar. Maybe just a few more chapters and then I'd go find him.

The sandwich had been sustaining. I put the empty plate and cup back outside the circle and returned to my work. I knew that I needed to be careful. If I wasn't, I could easily get sucked into this tangent and forget my training altogether. Because of this I made a pact with myself. I would only read a few more chapters then I go take a nap, or perhaps a bath, before finding Alexandar to resume our lessons. Having made up my mind I settled back into the chair. It somehow seemed less uncomfortable and more supporting now.

March 20, 1680

So much has happened. Within the first day of my travels I was beset upon by the Indians I feared. They tried to shoot me full of arrows, but I stopped them! It was astonishing the power that filled me at the meeting of my own demise. I knew I was meant for greater things but this was unbelievable. I. Stopped. Time.

The arrows were bearing down on me, just like the carriage was the child, and then they stopped. I pulled my arms down from the position they had assumed to protect myself and plucked the silent arrows from their frozen place in the air above me. I turned them away so that if they were to continue their flight, it would be to the ground.

*It took me a long time to restart what I had stopped. I ended up exhausted and shaking before I collapsed and time began again. The Indians had approached me and gazed at me as if I had two heads. One uttered a word: **Estanatlehi.** The others fell to their knees and helped me up. They took me and my supplies to their camp where I was give food, clothes, jewelry and women.*

From what I could gather they thought that I was a favorite of some Goddess they worshiped, the Goddess of the passing seasons. They took care of me while I recovered from whatever it was that I was suffering from and then sent with me a small band of warriors to see me to my destination. A lot of time has passed while I recovered, but now I have a company of my own to help see me to my destiny.

    J.R.

March 22, 1680

Spring is upon us and the warriors are restless. Though it has only been two days since we left their home it seems the language barrier has begun to wear on them. We have been beset upon by rival tribes twice now and it seems as if it will only continue. We have not lost a single warrior though. The dreams have been warning me before the attacks.

I believe this to be the reason they have not yet left me on this journey. They are always awed when I predict what we will see or encounter next. I have been following the landmarks I see in my mind and the farther I go, the more intense the pull. I have begun to see faces and I wonder if these are the people I am looking for.

A cloud has also descended upon my dreams. I have begun to see fighting and awful things the farther I go. I see Indians being tortured and extorted. I see things that I would rather leave unsaid. Things that make bile rise to my throat and burn the back of my mouth. I keep these visions to myself, but I promise that I will help these people. I do not care what the cost is to me, I will help them.

    J.R.

April 1, 1680

One of the warriors has taken sick and we have placed him in the back of the wagon. He was bitten by a snake as we walked and let out a horrifying scream. For a moment I was back in my dreams, witnessing the horrors that plague me nightly. I rushed to the man's side but the snake had already slithered away. His fellows wound a length of leather about the affected area and began sucking at the wound.

I watched as a discolored liquid poured out of the bite marks. They placed him in the back of the wagon to rest. We resumed our travels but he quickly turned ill. I fear he will not make it through this night. Why didn't I see this? I have seen everything so far that

*has been a threat to our party. Why would something that could
kill one of the warriors not be foretold to me in my dreams?
The warriors look at me as if I had kept this from them on
purpose and I wonder what they whisper about when they think I
am asleep. They do not feel the same pull as I do to continue on.
Now that they have lost one of their own, will they continue? Will
honor be enough reward for them? I hope so.
J.R.*

I stretched and set down the journal. I wanted to keep reading but I
also needed to keep the promise I'd made myself. I could always
read a little each day. There could be some secrets locked in these
journals that we needed. Nodding to myself I stood. My neck felt
pinched and my back was stiff. My stomach was rumbling even
though I'd just eaten.

I walked out of the circle and ran directly into Alexandar.

"What the hell were you doing?" Alexandar grabbed my arms
and shook me hard.

Shocked, I just stared at him.

"What is wrong with you?" He shook me again.

"What do you mean?" I broke his hold and shoved him back.
"I was reading, what's wrong with *you?*" I demanded.

"You were in there for three days!" He shouted at me.

"That's absurd," I walked past him and continued on toward
the exit.

"It's true," he told me. "I was worried."

The sincerity in his voice had me pausing. I mentally took
stock. I did seem fatigued beyond what should have been just a
few minutes of reading, and I was famished.

"Three days?" I turned back to him and he nodded.

"How is that possible?"

"I don't know," he shook his head. "But I think you need to be
careful when you're reading those journals. There could be
residual energy trapped in them from while he wrote."

"Only a few minutes passed for me," I rolled my neck to get
out the kinks that seemed to have taken up residence. "But my
body feels like it was sitting for an extended amount of time."

"So maybe it slows down the mind?" Alexandar caught up with me and we headed toward the door to the corridor.

"Perhaps some sort of comprehension retardation?" I frowned. "I'm a very fast reader. I only stood up after reading a few chapters because my stomach was telling me I needed to eat. I got up the second time because my back hurt. Interesting. You can spell objects with your Element in a way right? Like the books."

"In a way," Alexandar frowned.

"Then if this is the Time Elemental, or Time Warden as the Agent of the Void, called him," I theorized. "It's possible that he spelled the books to slow down time within that bubble when they are being read."

"That would make sense, I left you the first time for almost two hours and when I came back you were standing in exactly the same spot," Alexandar stated. "How much did you get through?"

"Several pages," I said. "Which normally takes me five minutes or so. That does not match up with the amount of pain and hunger my body was expressing."

"So five minutes in your time was three days outside the bubble," Alexandar concluded.

"It appears so," I sighed. "Looks like I won't be able to get through the journals as quickly as I was hoping then."

"No," Alexandar frowned.

"I'm starved," I yawned.

"You're probably exhausted as well," Alexandar ran his hand from my shoulder to elbow before letting go.

Fire shot through my veins at his casual touch. I'd never even had a friendship where someone was comfortable enough to touch me casually. It was disarming and had a blush creeping up my neck. At times it was hard to remember that I hadn't experienced as much as most girls my age. My sister had lost her virginity before graduating high school and had a family within a few years after that. For many women it was normal to forgo education and begin a family early in life. I wondered what life would have been like if Alexandar and I had been normal. Would he have even spoken to me? Or would he have treated me just like everyone else I knew?

Doubts plagued me and I pulled away from his touch. There was no way such a boy as handsome as him would have liked me if I hadn't been thrust into his life.

"Did you know that most latexes are made with a milk protein?" I asked him. I continued at the look of confusion on his face. "Yes, in fact that makes most condoms produced unusable by vegans."

Alexandar cocked his head and smirked at me. My face flamed as he chuckled and shook his head. When he turned into the dining room I kept going down the hall.

"I'm not hungry anymore," I waved and kept moving.

"Ok," he said. "Are you sure?"

I nodded and waved behind me.

"I'll see you in the morning then."

I could hear the frown in his voice but I was unconcerned. Did he even like me? Perhaps I had imagined the smoldering looks and tempestuous feelings I read in his eyes. Disgusted with myself, I pushed all thoughts of Alexandar from my mind and entered my room. I was still hungry but I couldn't eat in the dining room after that beautiful display of my awkwardness.

As I walked through the door I found a plate filled with food and a cup of water in front of the fireplace. I closed the door behind me and leaned against it, smiling. The food smelled wonderful and my mouth watered. I sat at the table and ate hungrily. When I was finished, I sighed and pushed back from the table.

"Thank you," I said to the room at large. I felt dumb talking to an empty room but I had a feeling that I was being watched again. Now that my hunger was sated I was very tired. I crawled into bed and kicked off my shoes, falling into a deep, dreamless slumber.

Knocking on my door is what woke me. I yawned and stretched. Feeling refreshed, I stood and noticed that the small table, chair and platter of food remnants was gone.

"Thank you again," I said before opening the door. Even if I was just talking to myself I felt it necessary to be polite.

"Thank you for what?" Alexandar asked.

"Never mind," I waved my hand to dismiss it, slightly embarrassed.

"Ready for training today?" Alexandar's smile seemed to glint.

"As I'll ever be," I gave him a tentative smile as the doubts that I had shut out with my bedroom door crept back in.

Over the next few weeks I jammed my head so full of information it was close to bursting. We took breaks only to visit the boys and eat. I could compare it to cramming for an exam, but because I had never procrastinated enough to warrant actual cramming I wasn't quite sure. Learning and knowledge retention always came easy to me. I was repeatedly surprised by the facts I was finding. This really was a whole new world and I had so many questions. Alexandar was there to answer all of them.

"Ok," Alexandar said in the middle of one of our session. "I think it's time to learn something new."

Abruptly he stood from where he was leaning against the chalkboard.

"New?" I shook my head. He spoke as if what I'd been learning was old news.

"You need to learn how to fight," he told me.

"I thought that was what we were doing," I stood and followed as he walked away from our little schooling area.

"You of all people should know practicum is not the same as practice," he shot over his shoulder. "Let's see what you've learned."

"Practicum is actually a supervised practical application of what you've learned," I mumbled to myself, then picked up the volume as he got further ahead. "They are in essence the same."

I heard his chuckle and picked up the pace.

The horror of middle school dodgeball flashed through my mind. I had always been the smallest and easiest to get out. The last to be picked to be on a team. The one ostracized for my lack of practical skills. I hurried after him. I've never had to protect myself before. The two times I had really used my Element I'd been in a haze. I had been able to control the air without thinking but now I needed to actually work on it. Before this life, I was a pacifist. I'm not sure that was an option anymore. Even with everything I've lost I still didn't want to fight. Not really.

Alexandar lead me to a large workout room with a big matted floor. Chauncy was at one of the machines, pumping iron. I'd never really considered that a way to describe lifting weights, but with how quickly and efficiently he pumped the bar up and down it definitely fit the brand. I dragged my feet as Alexandar walked to what looked like a wrestling area on the mat, complete with circles painted on it.

"Ok," he turned to face me. "Come at me."

"I don't understand," I frowned at him.

"I mean hit me," he chuckled.

"With my element?" I was having a hard time comprehending what he was implying.

"No," he laughed. "With your fists."

"Why?" I took a step back. "I thought we were going to practice fighting with our elements."

"You can't really understand how to fight with your element until you understand how to defend yourself physically," Alexandar dipped into some sort of fighting stance.

"I can't hit you," I took another step back.

"Sure you can," he took a few steps forward. "You just need to try."

I heard a metal clank and saw that Chauncy had taken a break. He watched the exchange with amusement lightning his eyes while he toweled the sweat from his face. I wracked my brain for anything I knew about fighting.

"Did you know that llamas are born with an extra set of teeth for fighting?" I asked him. "They are for castrating the competing males in the group so they can remain the only fertile one."

Chauncy and Alexandar seemed to share a look that was part amusement and part confusion. Alexandar rubbed his hands on his thighs.

"What if...," I cleared my throat. "What if I don't know how?"

"I guess you're about to find out," Alexandar lunged.

I squealed and jumped out of the way. Alexandar laughed and stalked me like a cat playing with his dinner. It was a series of bait and dodge while he followed my retreat around the room. Chauncy could no longer contain his amusement and guffawed loudly. The noise brought Valerie into the room where she leaned against the doorjamb, watching the scene unfold.

Soon I was out of breath from running and the giggles took over, which was when he grabbed me and squeezed. The light sparkled in his eyes and I noticed red flecks embedded in his irises. When his smile reached my own the looked changed and then his gaze flicked down to my lips. I held my breath. We hadn't kissed since before we took the boys to their new home. I closed my eyes and leaned in.

"Sorry to interrupt," Valerie coughed.

"Ah," Chauncy laughed. "They were just starting to get to the good part."

"Well I'm sure they weren't planning on a floor show," Valerie chastised.

"I guess we'll never know now," Alexandar grumbled and stepped back.

"I'm sure you'll find out soon enough," Valerie walked toward us, tongue in cheek.

"Did you find something?" Alexandar wanted to know.

"You could say that," Valerie chuckled. "While you two have been playing school, Chauncy and I have been working tirelessly to find something on the sword. And we finally came across something last night. We were just waiting for you guys to finish your studies. No wonder it took so long."

"I beg your pardon?" I reddened at the idea that I would focus on Alexandar rather than my studies. "I will have you know that I value knowledge above all, including pleasures of the flesh."

"It was a joke," Valerie laughed.

"Yeah Doc," Chauncy smiled and stood up from the machine. "We figured the whole island would shake when you guys got together and so far no quakes. Obviously that hasn't happened yet."

Alexandar just chuckled, but my face flamed even redder.

"While muscle spasms are common after an orgasm, I find it highly unlikely we would shake the island," I spoke into the silence. It didn't seem to help.

"What did you find?" I asked trying desperately to change the subject.

"Well, the sword is definitely made from the Elements," Valerie said.

"So you found it?" Alexandar asked.

"Sort of," Valerie hedged. "You have to come and see for yourself, but it's obvious you two need to finish whatever it is you started. The information has kept this long, a bit longer won't kill any of us."

I watched as they both left. Chauncy caught Valerie's hand and she smiled back at him. That was something I'd never really considered having, a relationship so easy it was like breathing.

"Let's start over," Alexandar's voice shook me from my reverie. "Let's start with stance."

He came up behind me and set his hands on my hips. I froze. The few times we'd kissed we'd broken apart before it could get much farther and I was surprised by his tenacity. I was surprised again when he repositioned my hips rather than pulling me against him. I bent my knees at his insistence and stood with my feet shoulder width apart.

Walking around the front, he took my arms and brought them up to cover my face.

"This is called your guard," he circled me making slight changes to my posture. "Show me how you make a fist."

I pulled in my thumbs and wrapped my fingers around them. When I held them out for his inspection he chuckled.

"That is a good way to get your thumbs broken," he said.

Taking my wrist, he opened my palm. He seemed to hesitate, then drew a line from my wrist to my middle finger. I shivered involuntarily at the fire it excited. He pushed my fingers down slowly, one at a time, and finished with wrapping my thumb on the outside of my closed hand. I felt more powerful just by holding my hands like this. I laughed awkwardly, trying to shake the feeling away. Self-Empowerment had never been a priority for me. Now that it had to be, I resisted. It felt wrong to empower myself. Alexandar was watching me closely.

"What's going through your mind?" He wondered.

"I'm not sure I can do this," I answered honestly.

"Are you giving up without trying?"

"Of course not," I frowned.

"Then you need to believe you can do this." He said as he touched my head. "This can be your greatest ally or your worst enemy."

"I don't want to hurt people," my throat felt raw and a lump was forming.

"That's the beauty of defending yourself," he smiled at me. "You can choose not to, but if you don't learn you won't have the tools when you do need them."

I nodded and took a deep breath. The bullies that I'd dealt with swam before my eyes. Would I have used self-defense on them if I'd known? Or would I have still let them beat me up? Would I still be a pacifist if I learn to defend myself? Or was my lack of knowledge what led me to dislike fighting in all forms?

I raised my fists back in front of me and swayed in the stance my like I'd seen Alexandar do. The swaying helped me find my balance.

"One more thing," he ran lightly to a corner and came back with a set of gloves for me and a large round pad for himself. "Let's start here and teach you the mechanics of a punch."

I nodded as I slipped on the gloves and tightened the straps. Alexandar explained in minute detail: the difference between a strong punch and weak one, how to make sure your stance and wrist were strong and finally to aim at the middle of your target. I wasn't sure why I was getting this achy anxiety as I stepped into the stance he'd shown me. I could barely listen to his instruction. The thought of punching anything was becoming increasingly frightening. Logically I knew he wouldn't be hurt. Why was I so resistant? Taking a deep breath I held up my arms and stared at the pad.

Suddenly, everything became clear as I cast the first punch. Every time I hit the pad I could see the people who had wronged me. People I never thought twice about. The pain was so raw it consumed me. My breathing became labored, my eyes stung and the lump grew full force in my throat. But I couldn't stop, the more I punched the more it flowed out of me.

Mr. Conrad. My middle school science teacher who had repeatedly attempted to belittle me because of my age and my sex. Charice Dixon. A girl in eighth grade who had become my friend only to tell me later that she had pretended on a dare. The bullies who had dogged me through high school. They'd thrown me in lockers and attempted to drown me once in P.E. My father. My mother. Finally, my sister. How dare she leave me? How could she? Why? Why me? This wasn't what I wanted.

Alexandar dropped the pad and caught me as I threw the last punch. I fell straight into his arms where we dropped to the ground and I sobbed into his shirt. I felt empty and helpless. The power that had coursed through my body with that first swing was so unspeakable I was completely inept at describing it. When I'd finally gotten my breathing under control, I could hear Alexandar murmuring to me in what I've assumed to be Gaelic. I turned my face into his neck and breathed in his scent.

It was intoxicating. A mixture of cut grass and a field after a fresh rain. His breathing caught as I lifted my lips to a spot under his ear. A new kind of power began coursing through me and I turned into him. I sat on his lap and explored the curve of his jaw. He seemed to go very still, as if moving would scare me away. I ran my hands down his arms and felt the jump of his muscles at my touch. When my hands reached the bottom of his shirt, I hesitated and looked into his moss green eyes he nodded. I pulled the shirt up and off and looked at his bare chest. The muscles were taught and the skin over them was scarred. I looked back into his eyes and there seemed to be a grim sense of understanding there.

Small round burn marks with small groupings like an odd correlation chart. Puckered skin from cuts seemed to crisscross his chest. A horror filled me. What had he suffered before being an Elemental? I leaned forward and kissed the closest grouping of burns. There was a sharp intake of breath from him then his hands were on me and he was kissing me.

My emotions were swirling as he pulled me closer and deepened the kiss. A fire had been ignited and I wasn't sure I wanted to put it out anymore. I had been empty after I'd poured my emotions into defending myself and now I needed something to fill myself again. I couldn't get enough of him. His hands were everywhere. I didn't even notice when the ground shook, but Alexandar did. He pulled away and put his forehead on mine, trying to catch his breath. I tried to pull him back but he resisted.

"You really want our first time to be on the gym floor?" He asked.

"Right now," I told him. "I couldn't care less."

I felt a shudder go through him and that power I'd felt at the beginning surged up again. I had the ability to seduce him. It was a heady feeling.

"And that is why we won't do this now," he told me. "Because I know you will care."

He stood and pulled me up with him.

"You need to get back on the horse," he told me picking up the round pad again. "Otherwise this will be harder next time."

Trepidation filled me as I looked at the pad. Would the same thing happen? Would I lose myself in my emotions again? I wasn't sure I could survive it a second time. I took the stance I'd been taught and took a deep breath. When I threw the first punch it didn't feel as draining. There was still a slow simmering boil below my skin for all the people that had ever wronged me in my life but as I threw another punch I realized something. I had forgiven them. All of them. My knees felt weak and I stumbled as I threw another punch. My breathing slowed again and I breathed deep. The resentment I'd been holding my entire life was gone. I hadn't even realized it was there. I didn't know there had been that underlying rage just below the surface. How often had I shoved it back? Pushed it down because it was the polite thing to do? No more.

When I stood up again I faced the pad and something else appeared in front of me. A new mission. I imagined a faceless character that needed to be defeated, something to work towards. When I punched again it was one step closer to my mission. Instead of rage I felt righteous.

 Alexandar had gone through different moves and punches with me for what felt like hours. Rather than drained afterward I felt invigorated. I had wanted to keep going but Alexandar convinced me to take a break. We were both covered in sweat and it was time to meet with Chauncy and Valerie to find out what they had learned about the mysterious sword that appeared in our latest battle.

"I have something else to show you first," he took my hand. "We have a bit of a hike."

"Ok," I smiled and swung our arms as we walked. "I feel like I could climb a mountain and still have some energy leftover."

When we got to the surface I realized that he had taken me seriously. The mountain, which sat in the middle of the island, rose above us. Winding upward was a small trail that looked relatively unused. Brush and bramble grew over the trail in areas, making it difficult to traverse. After a few miles we slowed and Alexandar put a finger to his lips. He moved forward and pulled aside some branches that had obscured the view ahead. I moved in closer to get a better view and was nearly blinded by the sun gleaming off the water.

Past the branches was a hidden lake surrounded by trees. Maple dominated the area with Pine dotted throughout. The air within this little alcove was still. A fine mist seemed to hang in the air and hovered over the water. I wanted to move into the clearing but Alexandar held me back. I looked at him and he pulled me down into a crouching position, then leaned in and whispered in my ear. His warm breath on my neck gave me goosebumps.

"Now that you've learned the basics of fighting with your fists," he said. "You need to learn how to do simple recon using your Element."

"Why are we whispering?" I asked.

"Close your eyes," he chuckled. "You'll find out in a moment."

I frowned but did as he asked.

"Your Element can tell you a lot more about your surroundings than you think," he continued. "Start with what's closest to you. Communicate with the Air surrounding us."

I wasn't sure what he meant. I huffed out a breath when nothing changed.

"You're thinking too hard," he said. "Just relax, find your center."

"What does that mean?" I huffed. "The center of the circulatory system is the heart. The center of the pulmonary system is the lungs. You want me to focus on those?"

"Sure," Alexandar chuckle.

"Ok," I frowned.

I took a deep breath, then another. I thought about how the air felt filling my lungs. The warmth when it left. Another deep breath and I could feel the air farther away. My eyes popped open when I suddenly heard Alexandar's breathing as if he were directly in my ear. As soon as my concentration was gone the sound moved away.

"Good," he said. "Now try to expand it."

I closed my eyes again and centered myself. When I felt Alexandar's breathing within me I moved past him to the clearing. The clearing was filled with breathing. From the insects that walked on the ground to the birds that lived in the trees. The wind that surrounded the island didn't seem to reach within this clearing. Then there was something that made me stop. It was a larger beast than the other beings around the clearing. It breathed heavier and seemed to sputter like a horse. I opened my eyes and looked toward the clearing again but the lake was empty.

"Where is it?" I whispered.

"About ten feet that way," he nodded his head without looking.

"Why can't I see it?" I frowned.

"Because you still won't let yourself believe," he shrugged.

"But I want to," I sighed.

"Then that's the first step," he smiled and touched my shoulder. "Now look again."

I looked toward the lake and just enjoyed the scenery. Why was I so resistant? I had accepted everything else, hadn't I? I suppose my biggest problem was with the existence of a race that I couldn't see. I had taken classes that had purported a separate reality that bordered on our own, a fifth dimension of sorts. How could something like that exist in reality? Even though it wasn't logical, I wanted to see it.

That's when I realized that I wanted it to be real. I wanted the fantasy. I wanted this life. Then, just like someone flipped a switch, I saw movement. It was grainy at first, like the fuzzing of an old television then it popped into focus. I could see the rippling muscles of a white steed. It bowed its head and drank from the lake, snorting at the water. Slowly, more seemed to move out of the mists and in my line of vision. There had to be at least twenty. My mouth fell open and I just gaped. I must have made a noise because the one closest turned and looked right at me. The beast threw its head back and snorted, then moved toward our hiding place. I did my best not to move. As it got closer I saw something shiny protruding from the center of its forehead. It was a horn, straight and silvery, shining in the gleaming sunlight. It was a unicorn. There were unicorns that lived on the island. My eyes burned. The fantasy was real.

The unicorn poked its head through our little window. It blew air into my face and I slowly lifted my hand. It shook its head back and forth and lipped my fingers. With a snort it turned and left. My tears fell freely. I knew now what we really fought for. Not just the lives of the people that lived on the planet below us but also for the lives that no one knew existed anymore. I shook myself and gave Alexandar a watery smile.

"Let's go," I took his hand in mine. "I finally understand."

We all piled into the "war room", as I had taken to calling it. Books were piled everywhere. Some lie open on top of piles, others were laid down open. There seemed to be an odd order to the chaos, almost as if one pile pointed to another. I stepped over and shimmied around so as not to disturb the organization design by a mad scientist. One pile rose so high it nearly touched the ten foot ceiling. I wondered how they'd accomplished that without a ladder, then I thought uncomfortably about a book sized version of *Jenga*.

When I approached the table I could see a few books lying face up with a shimmery gold glow, indicative of the talking books. Between everything that had happened to my family, my preoccupation, with training and the journals, I'd practically forgotten about the talking books. It seemed odd that I would forget a detail as impressive as that but these were the living details of my life now. It felt as normal as forgetting about bus stops or the existence of democracy, the details that most people take for granted in their everyday lives. It was sobering that I now considered talking books an everyday norm. My life had changed so drastically in such a short amount of time.

As we gathered around the table the room seemed to hum in anticipation. I wondered if the faeries had joined us, but as always I didn't see any. I would see flickers of movement from the corner of my eye, but when I looked the movement would be gone. It was an eerie experience. Something occurred to me that had a shiver running down my spine. What else existed that we didn't know about? With everything that I had found out in the last few months, what else would I learn about in the near future? A heavy sense of foreboding had me shaking away the feeling to concentrate on the task at hand.

Valerie walked to a specific pile of books. It seemed as if she had to hop, shimmy and limbo to get there, but who was I to judge. If I'd been the one doing the research more than likely the room would look much the same. I might have catalogued the shelves and repurposed them for the task, so that the sectioned books were perfectly organized and in order of use, but that would have been the big difference. Valerie cleared her throat, breaking my compulsive thoughts. I snapped back and realized that I was just about to touch some of the books. Folding my hands I walked toward the table and away from my obsessive organizational thoughts.

"Ok," Valerie smiled at me. "Now that we're all here we can get down to it."

"What is it?" Alexandar asked.

"It may be more appropriate to show you something first," Chauncy smiled.

As soon as he picked up the sword and dropped into a fighting stance the blade burst into flames. When he stood the flames went out and it looked just like a normal sword again. Valerie held out her hand and he handed it to her. She took up the same stance as Chauncy. Instead of flames, the sword grew shards of ice. She swung it at the table which dented with a loud clang, but the ice held with minimal chipping. Then she held it out to Alexandar. With a small hesitation he took the sword and, with a deep breath, assumed the same stance as the two before him. Nothing happened. He frowned.

Staring at the sword he shook it. Still nothing happened. Shrugging, he handed it to me. I sank into the now familiar stance and immediately all loose papers began blowing about the room. I slid fluidly out of the stance and the papers fluttered to the ground.

"Can I see that again?" Alexandar held out his hand and I put the sword, hilt first, in his hand. There was a split second while we both touched it that voices seemed to whisper around us. I looked at him and his frown deepened, like he could hear it too.

When he raised the sword out of my grasp the voices stopped abruptly. He sank into the ready pose again and there was still nothing. Standing, he set the sword on the table where it shined in the firelight.

"I had a feeling it would go that way," Valerie stated.

"Why?" Alexandar wanted to know.

"We found this passage in reference to the sword's conception," Chauncy set a glowing book down in the middle. "The reason it took us so long was that it's in Hebrew."

"Hebrew?" I asked. "Like the Torah?"

"Exactly," Valerie said. "So we needed a translator."

Chauncy set down another glowing book with a grim look.

"You didn't," Alexandar looked aghast when Chauncy nodded.

"We needed it," Chauncy told him. "There was no way we would have been able to translate this quickly without it."

"I don't understand," I interrupted. "What did he do?"

"I created a speaking book to translate the text for us," Chauncy replied.

"Why is that a problem?" I wondered.

"Because you have to leave a part of yourself within the book to give it the necessary life to function on its own," Alexandar was near to shouting. "What is wrong with you? Don't you remember why Moira chose the path she did?"

"I remember," Chauncy said.

"We could have gotten a translator up here!" Alexandar began pacing in the small space he had.

"At what cost?" Chauncy asked. "We probably would have gotten that person killed. I won't be a part of that anymore."

"What do you mean leave a part of yourself?" I asked.

"A literal piece of your soul," Alexandar said, pivoting angrily to look at me. "The thing that gives you life, that makes you, you."

"He's angry because Moira had created many speaking books before she turned," Chauncy watched Alexandar as he spoke. "And he's afraid I will do the same."

"Eventually she couldn't make them anymore," Alexandar said back to him. "Because she didn't have anything left inside. She couldn't tell the difference between good and evil anymore. Logic was all that was left."

Alexandar sat down with a thump.

"I should have seen it," he put his head in his hands. "I should have prevented it."

I kneeled down next to him and put a hand on his shoulder.

"What's done is done," I told him. "It's time to move on and stop beating yourself up about what you couldn't stop."

"That's easy for you to say," he said. "You didn't lose..."

He stopped and looked up at me. I couldn't blame him for forgetting. I'd almost forgotten myself. The things I'd lost, the people I'd lost. The mission is all that was keeping me sane at the moment. In any other setting I would have considered this an entertaining thought that the fantasy could keep me from remembering my family. But when I considered about what my reality now consisted of it just seemed hurtful.

"I'm sorry," Alexandar stood and pulled me in close.

I wanted to pull away but I knew he needed the comfort more than I did. I felt like I still needed to shut out the feelings for a bit but now that I remembered it was hard to close off the deep regrets and anger. Another reason to tear apart the Void. The sword seemed to shudder at my thoughts and edge closer to me.

When I looked over I saw that Valerie was watching me closely. I stepped away from Alexandar and smiled hollowly at him.

"What did you find?" I repeated the question of the night.

Instead of answering me directly, she smiled and addressed the book.

"What is the Angel's Sword," Valerie asked.

One book repeated the question in Hebrew, the other responded in the same language in which the first book repeated in English.

"The Angel's Sword is a weapon forged in the lava pits deep within the Earth and given life by the four Elements," it said.

"What Elements?" Valerie asked.

"Fire, Water, Air and Passage," it repeated after a moment.

"Passage?" I asked.

"Time," Chauncy answered.

"Why didn't Earth help?" I asked the book.

"The Element of Earth embodies life and renewal," the book answered. "The Element and the chosen Elemental refused to assist in creating a weapon to tip the balance of the world. The struggle between the Elements and the Void is a fact of life and death."

"That sounds foreboding," Alexandar frowned. "Why are we fighting if there's no winning?"

"You know why," Chauncy said.

Alexandar sighed and scrubbed a hand across his face.

"I need a break," he said and turned to leave. "Let me know if you find out anything I need to know."

I frowned after him as he walked out the door, knocking over a couple piles of books on his way out. I needed to get to the bottom of that but the information at hand was much too important to walk away from at the moment.

"Why is it called the Angel's Sword?" I asked the book.

"That nickname was created after stories were written about a flaming sword that guarded the entrance to a secret garden known as Eden," the book said. "The stories were reinforced when there was a very public fight between the Void and the Elementals in two cities called Sodom and Gomorrah."

"Are you telling me that the Angels in the Bible are actually Elementals?" The book didn't respond of course.

"I think that's the case," Chauncy nodded.

"How many swords were made?" I asked the book.

"Four," it replied.

"Where are they?"

"They were lost during a great battle," the book said. "In which every Elemental was killed."

"I wonder if Earth has changed its mind about the use of the sword since then," I mumbled, more to myself, but Valerie responded regardless.

"It's funny you should say that," she smiled. "Because we found something else while we were looking."

"Which Elementals died in the battle?" Chauncy asked the book,

"Fire, Air, Water, Earth, Passage, Pain, Vortex, Stratos, and Helix," the book responded.

"What were the last four?" I asked.

"We think they are the Agents of the Void," Chauncy could barely contain his excitement.

"Pain, Vortex, Stratos and Helix," I repeated. "But if everyone died, how was the information passed on?"

"We have a theory on that," Valerie looked to Chauncy.

"I told you that when all the Elementals die then one of the Elements takes human form for a short period of time to school the new Elemental right?" Chauncy scratched the back of his head as I nodded. "Did I mention that I was one of the most recent of those new Elementals? This has happened more than once in the past."

"You met an Element?" My mouth must have been hanging agape because he chuckled.

"Yes," he nodded. "I happened to come into my power at a time when the past Elementals had all been exterminated."

"What happened?"

"I don't know all the specifics," he looked around for a chair and sat. "Just that it was bad, really bad. He came to me as a missionary. At first I was resistant, of course, but once I began to believe he scooped me up and we came here. I found out that the Sanctuary was the only safe place for the Elements in their vulnerable form. After I learned the basics he tasked me with a mission: Find the others and learn together. It took a few years to get everyone together but we did it."

"You did it," Valerie walked over and wrapped her arms around his neck, leaning in.

"True," he smiled up into her eyes. Their love was so deep I could feel the echoing reverberations in the room.

"So," I cleared my throat. "What's your theory?"

"Oh," Chauncy blinked like he'd forgotten I was there. "Right."

Tongue in cheek, I smiled at them both. They seemed to be so wrapped up in each other they forgot what was happening around them.

"We think that when all the Agents die the Void must also take human form to pass on its information," Valerie laughed breathlessly. She could barely contain the information.

"But if that's the case," the wheels were turning in my mind. "Then we might be able to kill the Void."

"Exactly," Chauncy beamed at me like I was his prized pupil.

"I have to go tell Alexandar," I turned to leave. "This is amazing!"

I found him in the hot springs floating on his back. I watched as he let himself be cradled by the water.

A clear objective was all that our team seemed to be lacking. We knew we had to fight the Agents but it seemed to be a never ending fight. What if it didn't need to be? What if we could finish this fight? It was an exciting thought, that we could live normal lives again. What would that look like?

An image surfaced in my mind of myself, pregnant and laughing at something with Alexandar. A Nobel Prize sat on the mantel for quantum physics and its practical applications for everyday life. My research had been grounded in how the keys worked. Something I discovered during my time at the Sanctuary from studying the doors. I sighed as the image faded away. Who was I kidding? No life could be normal after this.

I stripped down to the bikini I was wearing under my clothes and joined him while he floated. I could tell he knew I was there but he didn't look over or acknowledge my presence. I shrugged and lifted my legs, treading water for a bit before I laid flat. The water covered my ears and I listened to the flow of the water and my own breathing. I closed my eyes and just floated. I felt movement next to me but ignored it. However, when I was lifted out of the pool and into his arms it was hard to pretend I didn't notice. I glared at him, but it was difficult to keep a straight face when he was looking at me so intensely. I burst out laughing, which didn't seem to please him overmuch.

"What's so funny?" Alexandar frowned.

"Just how serious we are," I sighed. "You know, most people our age are sneaking around getting drunk, having just started college."

He set me down in the water so I could stand on my own.

"Did you do a lot of partying in college?" He ran a hand through his wet hair. It hung near to his shoulders with the messy curls weighted down with water.

I wasn't sure why but that question struck me as particularly entertaining. I laughed so hard I inhaled water and began choking, which of course had Alexandar laughing as well. When I'd finally spewed the offending water and gained my breath back. I watched him laugh. My heart dropped into my stomach then jumped into my throat. It was pounding so loud I could feel it pulsing in my ears. This was the first time I had ever seen him completely at ease. There had been glimpses before like when I'd seen him playing in the music room. But this was pure, unadulterated joy bouncing around the room, and it was emanating from him. It made my heart sing. As corny as it sounds that was exactly how it felt, as if his genuine laughter ignited something within me.

Before he'd finished I moved over to him and put my hands on his shoulders. When he looked at me, the laughter still in his eyes, he smiled as I'd never seen him. I couldn't help myself. I covered my mouth with his and let the singing out. I kissed him with everything I had and hoped it would be enough. I wasn't sure what I was offering to him but it seemed like something very important. So when he pulled away and the longing warred with reason, I let him. I was hurt. I didn't know why. There was no logical reason to be hurt but my throat began to close and my eyes stung.

"Don't you want me?" I shuddered as tears leaked out against my will.

"You don't know how much," the seriousness was back and I ached for the light hearted Alexandar I had just seen. "Answer the question."

"What question?" I swiped at my eyes.

"Did you ever go partying?"

"No," I answered confused. "Of course not. I didn't have time for frivolities while I was getting my Doctorate."

"Have you ever been with anyone before?"

"No," dread tickled the back of my throat. "Why?"

"Let me finish," he sighed. "Have you ever been on a date before?"

"No," I looked down at my hands in the water.

"Before me," he paused. "Had you ever been kissed?"

"Not the way I wanted," the tears leaked freely as shame overwhelmed me.

"Look at me," he walked closer.

I refused to let him see the tears he'd caused, but he took my chin and forced me to look up anyway.

"I want more than just a heavy make out session from this," he told me. "I want to know you."

My heart stuttered in my chest at his words. No one had ever wanted to know me.

"I want to take you on a date," Alexandar smiled at me. "I want to court you. So stop making it so damn hard on me."

I let out a choked laugh and the tears ran free as he gently kissed me. Then he picked me up and took me out of the pool to dry off. I wasn't sure how to respond to what I'd just been told. Court me? I'd never been courted. I'd always been the weird girl who was too smart. Boys had flirted with me when they wanted something. There had even been a boy who'd kissed me sloppily. That hadn't ended well when I asked him about his kissing technique. I'd only wanted to learn, but he didn't see it that way.

I leaned my head on his shoulder as set me down. The scent from his skin was intoxicating. Because of the water currently smelled like freshly mowed grass after a rainstorm.

"What do I smell like?" I asked him.

He set me down and handed me a towel as he chuckled.

"Right now?" He asked and I nodded as I dried off. "A spring breeze blowing through a field of dandelions."

"Dandelions?" I smiled. "What do they smell like?"

"Exactly like you," he leaned in and kissed me lightly.

I frowned as something niggled at my memory then was gone again. Then my thoughts turned to the reason I'd come to find him.

"You know," I began as we walked out of the cavern. "Chauncy and Valerie think we can end the Void."

"Really?" Alexandar laughed. "How is that?"

"If we destroy all its agents it should take on a human form to pass on information," I said.

"It does that?" He wondered.

"That is the current working theory," I nodded. "Obviously we will need to test it."

He stopped and I realized my mistake.

"We have to kill all of the Agents for that to happen," he stated hollowly.

"Yes," I said. "She's not your sister anymore."

"How do you know that?" He said. "She spared our lives last time."

"And in the same breath threatened to kill us the next time she saw us," I lifted my brows at him.

"She's probably bluffing," he started moving again and pushed past me.

The air of easy camaraderie was gone and I sighed.

"But what if she's not?" I asked. "Would you test it with our lives?"

"No," he slowed.

"We will take this one step at a time," I told him. "Besides, I still need to learn how to fight."

"True," he said, tongue in cheek. "And that could take some time."

I punched him while he laughed.

The next few days were rigorous. Strength training, endurance training and lastly mental fortitude. The day would always start with Alexandar meeting me at the door of my room, both hands behind his back.

"Pick a hand," he would say.

Each day I would pick the same hand and each day there was nothing in it. He would laugh and ask why I didn't pick the other hand.

"Perseverance," I would reply. "Why is there nothing in your hand?"

He would just laugh and our day would begin. It was an odd but comforting routine. My muscles began to firm and my body became hard where it used to be soft. I wondered at the little dips and ridges that were taking shape. Once a week we would visit the boys, who always stood in stoic silence. Tad was usually the one to break and give me a hug and chatter on about his classes and the other children. Thomas would just nod or shake his head when spoken to. The only time he would make eye contact with me was when we were leaving and there were times that I wish it were otherwise. As soon as I would stand to leave or begin to say my goodbyes, his eyes locked on mine. There was a type of horrified betrayal locked within them, a kindling rage simmering before true ignition. His eyes would not leave mine until I closed the door behind me and I felt like I could breathe again. Every stare was a screaming accusation, telling me I was an awful person for leaving him there. Then one day he refused to see me.

Miss Wolfe said that he was fine and healthy but it was in his best interest to discontinue visiting. I didn't know what to say. I still visited like clockwork, hoping he would come around. Every time I walked in, though I was happy that Tad would run and greet me, I wondered what Thomas was doing and how he was.

As soon as I left after every visit I would remember that I had meant to ask about the financial aid I'd received for college. Then it was back to training. I was happy that there was little time to dwell on the situation. Finally, a day came that was different.

"Pick one," Alexandar said.

I picked his other hand. I was annoyed enough with this game to pick something else. When he opened his hand he smiled at my confused frown. His hand was empty.

"You're ready," he said, then abruptly turned and left.

"Wait," I hurried after him. "What am I ready for?"

"Something new," he chuckled.

When we entered the training room he didn't wait until I got to the mat before attacking.

"Keep up your guard," he yelled at me, it had become a familiar anthem. "They won't let you rest and now neither will I."

His punch came at my face quickly, which I dodged, but then his legs swept out and my feet were knocked from under me. I hit the ground hard and missed the mat. My backside ached but there was no time to think. Alexandar came in quickly from above and I just narrowly rolled out of the way before his fit hit the ground. To my horror the ground caved where he punched. He was using his element.

"That's not fair," my heart was beating in my throat. "You still haven't taught me how to fight with my element yet."

"Figure it out," was all he said before coming after me again.

I watched him as he moved. He seemed to use small things around him to give his punches, kicks, and even his movements, just a bit more of a boost. As I retreated he launched himself toward me. The very ground aided his movements; a push here, a brake there. It made them more fluid and solid at the same time. I'd watched a ballet once that had similar fluidity, though I doubted he would appreciate the comparison. By the time I'd finished the thought, I was back on my feet and he was hurdling toward me.

I threw up a wall of air just to give me a second but he blew through it, knocking me to the ground where he kneeled on my stomach painfully. I'd never seen him so focused before. His fist came flying at my face then whooshed to a stop, blowing the hair back from my face with the near impact. The tip of my nose was brushing his knuckle.

"You need to be ready," he huffed and stood up. "They won't stop."

"What's going on?" I struggled to my feet. "What's happened?"

"We got word that the Agents attempted to get to the Warren," he stretched his neck. "The boys are safe and the warren has moved, but this is a first."

"Do you think they followed us somehow?" My mind was reeling.

"It's a possibility," he nodded. "So we need to find out how they're following us. Plug the leak, so to speak."

"We may need to spend time in those tunnels," I agreed. "We could try and draw them out."

"Hmm," Alexandar's brows furrowed as he thought it over. I could tell a plan was forming.

"What are you thinking?" I asked.

"A work in progress," he smiled. "Now tell me what you learned."

We worked for the rest of the day. I found practical applications for my element while I was fighting. Ways that took little to no energy and boosted my movements. It was rocky going at first. There was a time I fell on my face, attempting to aid a jump. I gave myself just a little too much push and tripped over my own feet. Alexandar had laughed a long time before we got started again. My heart had done backflips. Even though that laughter had been at my expense it was a heart stopping experience and I loved every minute of it.

It helped that after he laughed he would hug me. Not an arm around the shoulder hug but a full body squeeze that had my head spinning. It told me that there was no negative intent with his laughter, just a shared experience and reassurance. I had experienced enough taunting laughter in my life to see the difference clearly, and it meant the world.

After we were done for the day I wondered when he would start courting me. It had been a few weeks since the conversation in the hot springs. Every day that he asked me to pick a hand, I had fantasized the item that resided in one of his hands that would begin our courtship. The heat between us was not dissipating and I wanted him to do something about it. The anticipation was distracting. When we met in the dining room for dinner later that day I was stunned to find the room clear of its normal heaping mounds of food. Next to the hearth was a tiny table for two. Domed metal covers topped the plates on either side of the tiny cafe table. Alexandar stood holding out my chair while I walked, mouth agape, toward him. He looked slightly less disheveled than normal. He even wore a tie over his polo shirt and khaki shorts. His feet were bare and I just had to laugh. I definitely did not feel underdressed in my flowing peasant top and jean shorts. My feet were also bare. It was oddly liberating to think that I hadn't worn shoes in weeks. I was learning new things at an incredible speed and at the same time I was more relaxed than I had been my entire life.

I sat in the chair offered and laughed as he pushed me in.

"Where are Chauncy and Valerie?" I asked.

"I told them the dining room was closed for the night," he chuckled as he sat, pretending to flip some non-existent coat tails behind him. "One day this will be a real date, in Paris or Rome. Anywhere you wanna go."

"This is pretty real right now," I smiled at him. "What made you start this today?"

He lifted the tops off the plates, letting the steam waft out. The scent was tantalizing. Lobster slathered in butter surrounded by field greens. I'd eaten something similar at a charity auction what seemed like a million years ago. With everything that had happened I almost wished for my old life. It was a lot simpler, if less fulfilling.

"You don't like lobster?" Alexandar asked as I was picking at my food.

"No, it's great," I took a bite and smiled. "I'm just tired. Sorry if I'm not that good of company tonight."

"You're the perfect company," he gave me one of those looks filled with heat and I felt my cheeks pinken.

"Come with me," he stood up, walked around the table and pulled out my chair.

I put my hand in his when he held it out and we walked out of the dining room, down the torch lit hallway and into the music room. He had me sit on the ground and he took a mandolin from the wall. Sitting next to me, he began to strum a tune. Slowly the room changed around us. Grass grew out of the floor, trees sprang up in an instant, the hammock I'd seen him in before was there again. The ceiling turned to a night sky filled with bright and shining stars that blanketed the darkness. A bright orange full moon shone its light into the valley that surrounded us. It was beautiful. Fireflies danced about the open field and I reached out as it landed on my hand. It fluttered lightly before taking off again. It felt so real. I could have been out in this field, a normal person enjoying a date.

"How is this possible?" I wanted to know.

"It's a little like astral projection," he continued playing and his voice took on a sing-song cadence, the timbre reverberating around me. "Except I bring the elements to me. You can touch and feel everything around you, but it's only here in spirit."

"Where is this place?" I sat on the grass and looked up at the starry night sky.

"A glen in Ireland near where I used to live," he began humming along with the music.

"Is this what you do when you get homesick?"

"Sometimes," he nodded. "I used to just pop down there sometimes, too. But now that they can find us so easily I wouldn't risk the people in such a small village."

"Why can't the Void find the island so easily then?" I laid back on the grass and closed my eyes, feeling the slight dampness of night and the cool breeze across my face.

"The island moves pretty quickly while it orbits," I heard the shrug in his words. "It's the only reason I can think of. They still make it onto the island occasionally, as you know."

"Yes I remember," I shuddered at the memory. "We should take the fight to them."

"When you're ready," he said. "We will. Now enough talk about the Void. Tell me something foolish you wished for as a child."

"Something foolish?" I repeated, laughing lightly. "I don't remember a time when there wasn't a serious book in my hand."

"Have you ever wondered why that was?"

"It never occurred to me to question my curiosity," I answered, then a memory long buried surfaced. "I wanted to be a dancer, but I was never graceful enough."

"I don't believe that," he said.

"It was something I was always told," I shrugged. "I just started believing it."

Abruptly, he set aside the instrument and stood. The scene vanished as quickly as it had appeared, and I was suddenly laying on the hard flooring of the music room. I was suddenly very homesick. He walked over and took my hand to help me to my feet.

"I have an idea," he said. "But we need to be quick."

"What's your idea?" I asked as he pulled me along behind him down the hallway.

"The Agents have no problem decimating small towns because it's usually chalked up to natural disaster when we fight," he announced as we hurried down the corridor.

"Ok..." I shook my head attempting to follow his train of thought.

"But we all avoid the main cities right?" He asked me.

"Right," I said. "Because we don't want to cause havoc and lose the lives in a large city."

"Of course," he said. "But that's our reason. Why don't they just attack a large city to draw us out?"

"What are you saying," I pulled him to a stop as we got to the portal doorway.

"I'm saying," he paused and took out his key. It glimmered in the torch light as it swung from his fingers. "That they won't attack us in a large public place because they don't want to be exposed. The Void thrives on chaos, if they are exposed the humans will unite against a common threat like they always do."

"You think that we would be safe in a large public place?" I asked. The thought that we could get out of the Sanctuary for a bit was intoxicating. I wasn't sure when, but I'd begun to feel like a prisoner here. Never seeing the sun or the sky it was stifling.

"You in?" He asked, holding out his hand for mine again.

"I'm in," I grinned at him.

"You only need two of the four keys to go somewhere," he told me, inserting his key. Then he stood back and motioned for mine.

I stepped up and felt the key warm in my hand. I pushed it into the slot and watched the door glow. Alexandar mumbled something to the door then opened it.

We stepped out into a dark room with thumping base. The door closed behind us to lasers danced and multicolored lights wheeling around the room. I'd heard of raves before but had never experienced one. The music was loud and the dancing fevered. The freedom was exhilarating. I caught Alexandar's grin as he pulled me onto the dance floor and it occurred to me why we'd come here. Because I'd wanted to dance.

"Why are we doing this?" I pulled him to a stop and had to shout in his ear. "We should be working."

"Because you need a break," he shouted back. "It seems it's been a lifetime coming."

His hair fell into his eyes as they laughed back at me. Who was this fun loving boy in front of me? Where had the serious man gone? I didn't have long to wonder before he pulled me into the crowd of bodies that took up the enormous dance floor. At first it was difficult to acclimate. In my previous life I would never even consider spending time in places like this. If I had to go to events with large numbers of people there I hung at the fringes, ready to bolt if I felt too uncomfortable. The press of bodies here made me cringe and my breathing became labored. Then Alexandar pulled me close and looked into my eyes. We could have been the only two there. Suddenly the press of bodies around me didn't seem so bad and the music wasn't as suffocating.

He wrapped my arms around his neck and we swayed together. I could feel the pulse of the bass in my chest and my heartbeat seemed to match the maddening pace. Our bodies moved together and every movement had my nerves tingling. I reached up to brush the hair out of his eyes and caress his cheek. His eyes were intense on mine as he seemed to consider something. I made the decision for him and leaned forward, resting my lips on his.

The tingling turned to fire and his hands pulled me closer. I let him explore my mouth and we moved together with the beat. My heart went from fluttering to pounding and my legs began to quiver. I had the urge to wrap myself around him. He pulled me from the crowd and we found a small dark corner just for us. My head hit the wall with a thump as he pushed me against it and I explored his mouth this time. His hands were everywhere as he pressed me into the wall. I lifted my leg and let him press farther. He moaned into my mouth, sending thrills down my spine. When his hands moved up my sides and cupped my breasts I shivered. The bass still pounded around us, adding vibrations to our movements. I wrapped my arms around him to bring him closer. Suddenly he wasn't there and I blinked in the darkness to find him.

As my eyes adjusted I saw that a fistfight had erupted around us and Alexandar had been knocked to the side. Fury exploded over his face as he pushed some drunk slob off and tried to grab my hand but the offender turned around and punched him. I squealed, ducking as a fist came at my face, and scrambled away. It occurred to me that I hadn't actually called for my element. The thought filled me with a sense of pride that I was capable of defending myself. When another wayward fist came my way I was about to stand my ground but someone caught it. A streak of dark hair and features dove into the fray. I stepped back and watched as this person fought with ease. When he turned my breath caught. Something inside me recognized him and I wasn't sure why. He winked at me then went back to fighting. When it was over he stood alone with Alexandar. They put up their fists as if they were about to fight each other.

"Wait!" I yelled.

Alexandar hesitated, looking toward me. The other man grinned and jabbed upward, catching him on the jaw and sending him into the wall. I gaped at the force. Alexandar wasn't down for the count though and popped right back up. I quickly made my way over to them and put my arms out.

"Stop!" I turned to the other man. "You heard me, why did you punch him?"

"Because he had his hands on you," the man grinned, showing off straight white teeth. It accentuated his dark eyes, slicked back hair and tanned skin. His accent was hard to place but I hadn't been around much, as I was beginning to understand.

"Why does that concern you?" I asked.

"Because you're my future wife," the grin widened as my jaw dropped.

"Gypsy scum," Alexandar spat from behind me. "She wouldn't marry you in a million years."

"We'll see," he leaned in close to whisper in my ear. "I read it in my cards and they never lie. They also told me who you really are and that I would be joining you soon."

Alexandar reached around me and pushed him away, taking my hand. The man waved as we retreated.

"See you soon!" He yelled after me, smiling.

A chill wound its way down my spine and I caught a glimpse of dark leather clad figures closing in. The man sensed this also and melted into the crowd. Alexandar made for the closest doorway and closed the door behind us. Inserting his key into the other side, we opened the door again and stepped back into the Sanctuary. We were greeted by the glowering expression of Chauncy's normally affable face. Something told me we were in trouble.

"What were you thinking?" He asked as soon as the door was closed, shutting out the thumping music. It suddenly seemed too quiet.

"We needed a break," Alexandar hunched his shoulders.

"Please tell me that wasn't a rave you were coming from," Chauncy looked skyward.

"I was testing a theory," Alexandar responded.

"What was your theory?" Chauncy demanded.

"That the Agents wouldn't cause a scene in an area with a large populace," Alexandar shrugged as if it were no big deal.

Chauncy just stared at him.

"You're telling me," Chauncy seemed to choke. "That you deemed other lives expendable to test your theory."

"Well when you put it that way," Alexandar frowned at him.

"What other way should I put it?" Chauncy demanded. "Maybe you don't seem to understand the gravity of the situation."

"No?" Alexandar asked. "Who have you lost lately?"

"Look," Chauncy massaged his temple. "I'm all for a break, but we are basically in a state of high alert right now. What would have happened if you'd been found, if you'd been captured or injured? Or what if your theory had been proven wrong? What if the Void had just swooped in and decimated the city? How could you be so reckless?"

"Well none of those things happened so it doesn't matter, does it?" Alexandar started to walk past him.

Chauncy touched his shoulder gently and Alexandar shrugged it off, continuing on. Guilt tore at my insides. I'd been so desperate to get out that I hadn't even given much thought to the consequences of my actions. Alexandar had made it sound like the risks were few and the gain was much higher. In reality, what had we gained versus the actual risk? A make out session and a fist fight that could easily have gone south. What about that prophecy from the mysterious gypsy? In order for him to join us, someone would need to die. I shuddered again as dread settled around me.

"I'm sorry Chauncy," I walked over and took his hand. "It wasn't my intention to cause problems. It won't happen again."

"Don't get me wrong, Doc," Chauncy smiled down at me. "I want you to have fun, it seems like you've had too little in your short life, but we need to stick close to home right now."

"I understand," I nodded.

"I know you do," Chauncy said. "I know he does too. He's caught in a spiral and you're helping him forget about his loss. I need your help to guide it in a more constructive way. When things calm down, we may be able to take a break somewhere."

"Really?" My laugh sounded more than a little hopeless. "We may need to steal time while we can, it could be the only way we get real breaks."

I walked away, the weight of what the man in the club had said to me heavy on my shoulders. It seemed unlikely that what he said was genuine, but if he spoke the truth then we all needed to be very careful.

 The next day Alexandar greeted me at my door like always, but now there was no longer a playful hand-behind-the-back game. He barely even had a smile for me, just a nod and then moved on.

Training proceeded as normal but without the playful undertones of the last month. The serious boy was back and I wasn't sure what to do with him. I didn't realize how attached I'd become to the Alexandar that would hold my hand in between bouts or checked on me if I went down hard.

"Get up," Alexandar danced back and forth while I struggled to breathe on the ground.

Sweat poured down my face and back, my muscles ached. He had never pushed me this hard in training before.

"I'm done," I waved him off, struggled to stand.

"No, you're not," he took a step forward. "Get up."

"I said I'm done," I managed to get to my feet and attempted to limp away.

"And I said you're not," he pushed me.

I was so tired, I tripped. I was horrified. No one treated me like this, let alone someone I thought I cared for. I was caught between the need to scream and cry. I just laid there trying to decide which. Alexandar poked me with his toe.

"You alive?"

"No," I mumbled into the mat. "Why are you doing this?"

"I told you yesterday I wasn't taking it easy on you," I could hear the petulance in his voice. I wanted so badly to be angry, but what he said was true. I could also tell that he was baiting me. He wanted me to fight him, wanted to be hurt. More than likely he was hurting inside, but I didn't have to take the brunt of his emotional turmoil.

I looked up at him. He was crouched down, ready for my outburst of rage. Unluckily for him, it wasn't coming. Something that I'd realized over the last few months, especially after he taught me how to defend myself, was that the rage I'd pushed down my entire life was there because I'd been afraid. The knowledge of that fact was freeing. I took a deep breath and just looked at him. Sweat was pouring down his face. His shirt was soaked and he looked exhausted. How much had he slept during the last month? What had he eaten? I'd been so concerned with myself that I'd lost sight of the people supporting me. It finally felt like it was the time to stand on my own. So I stood.

"I said I'm done," I took a stance and the air seemed to bend around me. I didn't hit him, but I connected with my element and it reinforced my will.

"So you are," he straightened. "Come with me."

We went skyward, through the hatch and above the Sanctuary. The wind was billowing around us. I bent it so that it continued on its way but gave us a small birth as we moved. Connecting with the air around me made it feel more like a tickling breeze that the hurricane it had seemed to be just seconds ago. As we walked in silence through the cold sunlight of early dawn there was still something preventing Alexandar from touching me and it was becoming disconcerting. My skin felt cold and clammy on the surface and I wondered why we were here.

"Why can't the Void come here?" He asked me.

"You said they could find this place," I turned my face to the sun and enjoyed the light play behind my eyelids.

"Yes," he said. "They can find it. So why aren't we attacked here on a normal basis?"

I frowned. That thought had occurred to me but when the attacks never came I had assumed there was a reason.

"Because we are in the stratosphere?" I guessed.

"Yep," he nodded, still unsmiling.

"But why would that keep them out?" I asked. "And how was I attacked here then?"

"The stratosphere is an area that exists between the void and the Earth's atmosphere," he intoned, as if lecturing.

"Yes," I scoffed. "I don't need a science lesson, thanks. Why would that keep us away from the Agents?"

"The Agents can exist within and without, but not in between," he began walking again. "They feed off of chaos. There is nothing but order in the stratosphere. It is in perfect harmony, so the only time they can set foot on the island is when chaos emerges, usually after a new person is Chosen. This floating island is almost always in perfect harmony, balancing between worlds."

He sighed and pulled a hand through his hair.

"They feed on chaos," he said. "So when they cause it, they get powerful as well. We never should have tested them last night."

"It was a sound theory," I said lamely.

"Yes, and it could have gotten a lot of people killed," he began walking again, a hand on his neck pushing at the tension that resided there. "We were lucky last night. You distract me. Badly."

"Is that why you've been avoiding my touch?" I asked.

"Partly," he nodded and I followed him. "There's something else I need to show you."

We walked for a while under the trees that somehow grew straight up despite the winds constant battery. Eventually we came to a waterfall at the base of the mountain surrounded by a boiling pit of lava, like a mote. It now made sense why the hot springs existed. Abruptly he turned to me.

"Find your center," he said. "You need to feel the island with your element."

There was that phrase again. I frowned but did as he asked, closing my eyes and silencing the worry that clouded my thoughts, I breathed deep and reached out to my element. I could feel the air around me move and sway. As I breathed deeper my element filled me and seemed to be eager to help.

"Good," I heard Alexandar say. "Now pretend your element is an extension of you. Reach out with it and feel your environment."

I swept out my arms and it felt like they stretched on for acres. I felt the leaves on the trees, the pine needles on the ground, the bark of exposed roots. Everywhere the air touched, I touched. I felt the steam rise around the water and the deepest part of the cave. I gasped and opened my eyes.

Alexandar nodded.

"They live here?" I asked.

"There are more. Keep looking. This is a chance for you to stretch your wings and see that your Elemental scope is near limitless."

I reached out across the island and found all sorts of creatures. I could see them in my mind's eye by their touch. There was one I came across that I just had to see. I opened my eyes and began hiking up the mountain. It was hard work but I knew it would be worth it. I now knew that unicorns weren't the only mythological creatures residing here.

Alexandar followed me up the side of the mountain. By the time I reached the top the sun was directly above us and the air was so thin I could barely catch my breath. Sweat coated my skin and I was exhausted. But the sight there was worth all of the trouble. I dropped to the ground, giddy. I couldn't help but laugh as I watched them play.

The small creatures played an odd game of hide and go seek. They ranged in size from the palm of my hand to the length of a common house cat. Their body types varied drastically and they all had beautifully colored wings. These were the faeries I'd expected when I'd heard the word. The field in which they played glowed in the morning light. The grass was calf length but could hide them easily, so they would pop out and startle each other. Their giggles were infectious. I found myself laughing aloud at their antics.

One particularly overweight faerie, about the size of a large and happy house cat, struggled to fly. I could only guess at the sex of the creature, but he had the look of a male. He would run lightly on the ground, more quickly than expected for his size, and when another faerie would pop out of the grass he would squeal in delight and hug them. Then he would let them go and the game would start again. There was no judgement with their faeries, they played regardless of size, shape or demeanor.

After a while, my laughter drew the large one over to me. He was curious at first, then he crawled right into my lap and gave me a hug. Tears stung my eyes. No judgement from the faeries. When he stood, he tugged on my hair to pull my face closer to him and whispered in my ear. It was completely incompressible babble, but he was so proud of himself he clapped his hands and gave me a wet smacking kiss on my cheek. I smiled at him as he ran back to his friends.

We hiked in silence back down the mountain. I could feel that Alexandar wanted to ask me something but I ignored it until we were near the bottom. I was tired mentally from the experiences I'd had today, and physically from everything else. I just wanted to get some rest.

"What were those called?" I asked Alexandar after a long time.

"They are the Sylphs," he responded.

The silence continued.

"What did he say to you?" Alexandar finally spit it out when we reached the bottom.

"The Sylph?" I stopped in my tracks, confused. "I couldn't understand him."

"No," Alexandar gritted his teeth. "The gypsy."

"The man from the bar?" I asked. "How do you know he was a gypsy?"

"Trust me," he said. "I know. What did he say to you?"

"Well," I cleared my throat. "He said that he would be joining us soon."

"That's all?" Alexandar's brows furrowed. I could feel him trying to read my expression.

"What else would there be?" I asked avoiding the truth. I wasn't sure why I was compelled to lie. I wanted to tell him about the vow of marriage but I was trying not to take it seriously myself. Something told me that telling him right now would be a bad idea. "Don't they prefer Travelyr?"

"I could care less what they prefer," Alexandar spat and continued walking. "Did he give you a timeline?"

"Just 'soon'," I hurried after him. "What's your problem with gypsies?"

"It's not important," he waved a hand.

"Aren't you worried what this means?" I asked.

"Soon doesn't necessarily mean immediate," he sighed and stopped. "I'm sorry that I've been so distant. I had a very bad experience with *Travelyrs* in the past."

Alexandar seemed to have a difficult time getting the word out.

"Seeing him talk to you brought up some bad memories, ones I don't want to get into right now," he cut me off before I could ask again then took my hand. "We live with death every day. I can't bother wasting time being upset about things that don't matter. You matter to me."

My heart squeezed. I mattered.

"You matter to me too," I took his other hand and put it up to my cheek, feeling the calluses.

We stayed like that for a while, taking comfort in each other's closeness. Finally we went back to the island port hole to the underside. As we neared the entrance something glittered and caught my eye. I frowned and bent over to pick it up. It was a compact disc case with a note written on it.

No time like the present, bring the sword and follow the instructions on the disc.

There were coordinates listed on the disc below the message. I looked at Alexandar and we exchanged looks of dread.

We found Chauncy and Valerie in the War Room.

"You're just in time," Chauncy looked up. "We think we may have found a way to create new weapons, but you're not gonna like it."

"No time," Alexandar said as we walked in. "We've got a problem."

"What happened?" Valerie held her breath as abject horror played across her face. "Is it the Warren?"

"No," I gave her a reassuring smile. "At least, I don't think so. We'll have to see."

I nodded at Alexandar, who popped the Compact Disc into a portable player sitting on a shelf.

"Tabitha," my adoptive mother's voice played through the speakers and the dread near strangled me. "They are telling me that you're my only hope. I find that hard to believe, but there you go. Though they also say that you are the reason they are holding your father and I. That I *can* believe. I tried telling them that you won't care. That you're the most disrespectful daughter in the history of families, but they seem to think that you will come save us. They told me that they tried to get to our grandsons and now I realize why you hid them. Good for you."

What sounded like a slapping sound and a gasp came from the speakers.

"If you don't come get us I understand," she spit something out and it sounded like it skittered across a table. "But they say they won't stop looking for the boys and that they will kill us unless you come to them. I'm sorry."

The apology came out as a choked sob before there was another slapping sound. The speakers cracked, signaling the end. I sighed when everyone turned to me after it ended.

"Were there directions?" Valerie asked.

I held up the jewel case.

"You all don't have to come with me," I smiled at them. "I have to get them out of there."

"You think that little of us?" Chauncy's voice was dangerously quiet. "You think that we would abandon you so easily?"

"Someone could die," the gypsy's dark, intense eyes swam in front of my own and his unintentional warning floated through my brain.

"We take that risk every time we leave the Sanctuary," he said quietly. "This is no different."

Valerie stepped to Chauncy and took his hand.

"We're in," Valerie smiled at Chauncy.

I looked at Alexandar and I almost dreaded his answer.

"You should already know what my answer is," he grinned at me.

I did know, which is why I was upset. I didn't want to lose him so soon after meeting him. My heart tripped a beat. It was obvious to me, with the information I now had, that he would be the one to die tonight. What other reason would the man from the club think that he would marry me, unless Alexandar wasn't in the picture?

I tried to return his smile but a heavy feeling settled into my stomach.

"Well," Chauncy smiled at me. "Time to suit up."

"Suiting up" seemed to just be putting shoes on really. I never consciously realized, but no one wore shoes here. It was much more comfortable but now shoes seemed to be constraining. Chauncy brought me the sword and I strapped it on. The others stood unarmed and I now had a prevailing sense of foreboding. Alexandar smiled at me reassuringly and I took his hand. I had just begun to experience the feelings that he could evoke, I couldn't bear to lose him now. Was this love? There was a shooting pain in my chest at the thought that he may not come home with me.

"I don't want you to come," I told him, firming my lower lip to stop it from trembling.

"Why is that?" He seemed to be holding back a smile.

"This is serious," I told him.

"Of course it is," he cleared his throat and schooled his face into harsh lines.

"That's not funny," I told him and his frown tilted up fractionally.

"I'm going," he shrugged. "Did you forget who taught you to fight?"

"Of course not," I told him.

"Well I guess it's settled then," he laughed. "You're staying behind. I don't think you're ready."

"That doesn't make sense," my brow furrowed at his logic. "I have to be there to rescue them."

"Everyone's going," Chauncy cut in. "We take risks every day but we fight as a team. Get used to it."

The weight of the sword on my hip felt unfamiliar. I felt ridiculous. I should have at least practiced with the sword before taking it into battle. I chuckled, the thought of me going into battle was absolutely ridiculous. I suppose that the thought of a nineteen-year-old Doctorate was likely just as ridiculous to some people, though.

"What's the plan?" I asked.

"We are going to split up into two groups," Chauncy said. "There are four of them and they usually work separately, so it's possible we will only be fighting one."

"Possible," I said. "But not probable."

"Correct," Chauncy said. "Which is why we will assume they will all be there. We will get close and let Alexandar search the grounds."

"As in search through his element?" I asked.

"Yes," he said.

"That's the plan?" I waited for more.

"Well we can't really make a plan until we know what's waiting for us," Chauncy seemed annoyed at my criticism.

"I have an idea," I grinned as a thought occurred to me. "Follow me."

I lead them to the key portal. Inserting our keys we went through my closet doorway. It seemed like a lifetime ago when we last used the portal to enter my townhouse. The place was still a mess, but was now covered in a layer of dust. I walked over to my trusty desk and found my computer, smashed. The wind went out of my sails until I remembered my tablet.

Downstairs was no better. The fridge door hung off its hinges and it seemed that the electricity had been turned off, as no one was here to pay it. I wondered what my coworkers thought about what had happened to me. They probably just assumed I'd gone off the deep end because I was so young. And to be fair, for a while, I thought I had. So why would I be surprised if that's what they thought too?

The living room was as much of a mess as everywhere else. I found my wayward tablet behind a tipped over armoire and powered it up, thanking all that was Holy that it still had some juice left.

"Ok," I tapped a few buttons on the touchscreen and brought up Google Earth.

I entered in the coordinates and found what looked like an abandoned warehouse in the middle of a small town. Looking at our battleground like this made the thought of what we had to do even more unrealistic. The weight of what we were risking had me wavering on whether we should even help my adoptive parents. My mother had never approved of me, and as nice of a parting letter that my adoptive father had given me I wasn't sure it really made up for the way I'd been treated. But there was a voice in the back of my head asking if I would be able to live with myself if they were killed. Would I? No. I would always choose life over the casual dismissal of anyone's existence.

I looked back at the picture of the warehouse. Tire tracks went in and out through the fence that seemed to surround it at only one point. It reminded me of the war games I used to play on the computer. I sat forward and ignored the low battery warning that popped up. A plan began to form in my mind as Looking at the entrances and exits. I looked at the three people surrounding me, I grinned. "Alright, here's the plan."

Once everything had been laid out for the group, there had been some initial arguments mostly from Alexandar. The loudest however came from a surprising place, Chauncy.

"You need to be sure," he said. "A lot can go wrong. What happens if you can't find your parents? What happens if you're attacked?"

"I think I have an idea," Valerie responded. "First, we need to have faith in each other. Second, I found something in the books that might help with at least one of the 'what ifs'."

The practical applications for strategy are not your forte, a nasty little voice whispered inside my head.

I've taken classes in philosophy, psychology, geology, geography and anthropology. None of those studies could translate appropriately to help me achieve my goal. As I approached the outskirts of the abandoned warehouse it now seemed glaringly obvious that I was the wrong person for the job. What had I been thinking? The sword banged against my hip with every step, reminding me why I was there, and why I was alone.

My friends. It was still a hard word for me to comprehend. The words felt awkward on my tongue and in my mind. My friends had not been receptive to my plan but none were able to offer a better strategy. Alexandar had looked at me with horror and frustration, demanding that he take my place. I'd explained to him multiple times why it had to be me. Finally, after Chauncy had placed a hand on his shoulder, he subsided into muted mumblings. Valerie's faith in me and her contingency strategy had been genius. Occasionally, as we'd prepared for what was to come, I would catch a glimmer of his silent anger. He was mumbling in his native tongue so I was unable to translate, but the tenor was clear. He was furious. I made a mental note to learn Gaelic if I returned from this battle.

The 'spell', as Valerie called it, was above and beyond anything I'd learned yet. It was old magyk, she'd told me. Something they still didn't know enough about. It seemed to be a powerful weapon, so I knew next where I would be focusing my studies. It had been a challenge, but a challenge I had been able to meet. Chauncy had been impressed and I'd glowed under his praise. I hoped everything would go as we'd planned, but if it didn't we were prepared.

The chain link fence looked like it was sagging in defeat as I approached and I prayed to whoever would listen that it wasn't an omen. A crack of thunder off in the distance had the hair on my arms standing straight up. Something felt off but I couldn't discern the cause. I knew I was walking into a trap. There was a possibility that my own self-preservation instincts were kicking in, but I knew what I needed to do. Taking a deep breath, I stepped across the point of no return and entered the abandoned compound. My heart beat hard against my ribs making it hard to hear anything else. I stopped in my tracks as it dawned on me. There was no sound.

Not one sound since I entered the compound. I no longer even heard the storm as it raced across the valley. I could see the light flash across the sky, silhouetting the surrounding hills. The area was shrouded within an eerie and unnatural silence that seemed to permeate the air. The smell of ozone was fierce and burned my nose and throat. I trudged on toward my target and stood before a large sliding door. The enormity of the building seemed like it may have been an aircraft hangar in the not so distant past. The door was gaping open and unsecured.

"Moira!" I grabbed the hilt of my sword. "Face me!"

I stood there for a moment and waited. Nothing.

"Hello?" I called into the cavernous dark.

A giggle came from behind me and I whirled. My hand convulsed around the sword. A doppelganger stood where I had expected Moira. Its face split in a nausea inducing grin that almost toppled its head off its shoulders. The grayish, blotchy skin shone like wet rubber in the dying light. A flash lit the sky and echoed off the dark marbles that must have been its eyes. They sat deep within its face, sunken and hollow.

"Decided not to wear my dead family anymore?" I asked the thing that stood before me. "Where's Moira?"

"You could say she's putting her face on," it giggled again and sent shivers up my spine.

The giggle was completely out of place and it made my stomach turn. It was the sound of a young child, truly amused.

I heard a low female chuckle and my blood ran cold. I turned around slowly to face Moira and the possibility of my doom. Plastering a mean smile on my face I breathed deep.

"Your brother says hey," I mimicked the way girls had spoken to me in high school. With a careless toss of my hair I looked at my nails. This was a role I had never thought to play. I tried for nonchalance as I turned to make sure the Doppelganger wasn't taking advantage of the fact I'd shown in my back.

"He does, does he?" Moira seemed to struggle with her facial features.

"Yeah," I laughed without feeling. "He's hopelessly in love with me."

Did it seem like her face was melting? It was uncomfortable to watch without staring, so I pretended not to care. Which wasn't hard since the Doppelganger was circling like a shark. Its movements were awkward and I could hear the snapping of its tendons with every step.

"Why are you telling me this?" Her teeth seemed to clamp together, and her jaw flexed.

"Because they're on their way and I want my parents freed," I told her. "So you can take me as bait and it will torture him. That's what you want right?"

A slow smile split her face unnaturally, it looked like her head might roll off her body. I did my best not to shudder but some of my disgust must have eked through. She walked up to me quickly. Walking may be a relative term when describing the way she moved. Her movement had spiders crawling up my spine while she advanced. I'd only ever seen them float before, not move on their own. The stilted, jarring movements reminded me of a Japanese horror film I'd watched under duress when I was younger. Like a marionette with an inexperienced puppeteer they seemed surreal.

When she reached me she leaned over and sniffed.

"Something's not right," she hissed.

Moira made some gesture with her hand and two more Agents revealed themselves. Both had unconscious bodies thrown over their shoulders.

"Are they alive?" I asked curiously. "Before I hand over the sword I want confirmation."

Moira smiled cruelly and made another gesture with her hands. The two Agents that held my adoptive parents dropped them on the ground, where they both groaned.

"That's good then," I looked at Moira.

I stiffened my spine and walked toward the lumps on the ground. It took all of my acting ability to avoid revealing how terrified I was really was. Every step felt like an eternity. Finally, I walked directly between the two Agents and checked my parent's pulses. When I confirmed that they were indeed alive, I sighed in relief. Taking both their limp hands released the focus on my projection. In that instant, a screech broke the silence around us and something heavy fell onto my back.

I managed to barely block the blow when we surfaced, but she followed it with an elbow that made contact with my cheekbone. I knew there was no way I could win this fight, not the way I wanted. I had done my best to just bring my parents with me, but it was time for plan B and I hoped my friends were ready. I didn't give them as much time as I had planned. With the next blow I grabbed her wrist and used her momentum to pull her down with me. Something I had learned from Alexandar.

As I lay on top of an Agent of the Void, I had time to consider the life I was now living. I never really thought about my death much. I'd always considered death an end unfitting for the life we live, especially for those that burn brightest. How can it just end in nothingness? That a person, that light inside them, can just cease one day. I don't believe in heaven or hell because it makes what you do in this life somewhat inconsequential. You shouldn't do something because you'll get the easy life after you die, you should do it because it's the right thing. You should do it to make yourself feel good.

Moira growled and pushed her face into mine, breaking my reverie. Her breath smelled of rotten garbage on a hot day. I opened my eyes to assess the situation. I still held a now screaming Agent of the Void, but we were back with my friends. I handed her to Alexandar, wrists bound with air. He then bound her hands further with his own element.

"We need to hurry," Alexandar took hold of his sister, his eyes grave.

I jumped away as Alexandar managed to push her into a chair. We immediately created rings of our Elements together around her, much to her chagrin. The cell was something that we did our best to practice before I left on my astral journey, but there was no way to know for sure if it would work. She began swearing, and I realized it sounded identical to how Alexandar streamed his curses.

When I looked at him the corners of his mouth tipped upward just slightly, as if he were reliving a favored memory.

"How did you know the Astral Projection would work?" Valerie came up behind me after she'd added her own Element.

"I didn't," I chuckled lightly then winced at the tenderness in my cheek. "It was something that Alexandar had told me when he started teaching me to defend myself. 'You bring things back with you, Good or Bad.'"

"Well it's good you worked so quickly," she put a hand on my shoulder. "He was about to pull you out when we heard her tackle you. I was glad we'd worked on this binding spell before you left. We still know so little about our Elements it's surprising we've lasted as long as we have. It was luck that we found this abandoned building nearby the coordinates. Did you see any more Agents?"

"Yes," I said. "Two."

By now my parents were groggily getting to their feet. Valerie hustled them out the door and closed it behind them. I had only meant to bring my parents with, but we'd been prepared for Moira in case they had not been there.

I gazed back at our Elements as they wove together to lock in the vacuum. It was an interesting idea, seeing as vacuums could only exist in confined spaces. Similar to trapping her within her own element, combining our Elements created a vacuum tight space. It was the main reason we'd decided on this specific weaving of our elements. A thought occurred to me.

"Why didn't my cheek heal like my hand did when I was first Chosen?" I asked.

"Because the faeries haven't had a look at you yet," Valerie winked.

Before I could ask what she meant by that, Chauncy interrupted.

"We need to adjust our Elements just enough so her head, and only her head, breaks through. Then we can talk to her," Chauncy announced to the room.

We each took a place in a circle around Moira and together we bent our Elements. The control made my face ache.

"Alright, Alexandar," Chauncy shook his head. "You know what we need to do now."

"We aren't going to kill her," Alexandar shook his head.

"Alex," Moira said in a pleading tone. "They're going to hurt me."

"I won't let them," he stated. "But you need to prove to us that you can reform."

"Of course," she said. "Just give me a chance."

"We aren't letting her out," I glared at Alexandar.

"Everyone makes mistakes when they're under the influence right?" Alexandar seemed to be pleading for me to understand.

"You think murder is a mistake?" I wanted to scream. "She's an Agent of the Void. There's no coming back from that."

"How do you know?" Alexandar spat. "Just because it's never been done before doesn't mean it can't be."

"Right," I frowned at him. "I know how important she is to you Alexandar, but she doesn't want to reform. It's obvious. There is only one solution. Think about it logically, not emotionally."

"It's not an option," he crossed his arms stubbornly.

"So what do you expect us to do?" Valerie chimed in. "Hold this forever? That's what is not an option Alex."

"How are you finding future Elementals?" I asked.

"Oh, Tabs..." She tried to smile despite her constraints. "I can call you Tabs right? I mean we may as well be sisters."

"Stop," Alexandar commanded. "Mo, answer the question. If you really want to be redeemed, prove it."

A war seemed to break across her face until she decided.

"I have it on me." Every word seemed to be forced, like something was trying to keep her from talking. Her facial muscles were twitching and her breathing was ragged.

"What is it?" I asked.

"A key," she choked.

"Who's key?" I desperately wanted to hear the answer.

"The Key of Passage." she said before she seemed to lose consciousness. The only thing holding her up was the jail we'd created.

"Did you hear that?" I turned excited.

"See," Alexandar said. "She can be redeemed."

He looked over and smiled at me. When our eyes met, it felt like we may be able to get through this.

"Watch out!" Chauncy pushed Alexandar out of the way as Moira shot a hand out of the Elemental binding, armed with a long curved dagger. It caught him directly in between his ribcage. As soon as the blade found its home everything seemed to speed up. I reached for the sword still at my hip. The Elements faltered around us as we lost our focus. Moira moved at top speed. She sunk the dagger to the hilt into Chauncy's chest, then she grabbed Alexandar. Valerie let out a keening wail as Chauncy fell to the ground.

I turned to see Alexandar and Moira disappear into a chasm that opened up beneath them. I ran to Chauncy and kneeled next to him.

Valerie's scream cut the night and reverberated in my chest. My heart squeezed. The dagger still sheathed in his chest, heaved with his slowing breaths. Blood poured onto the ground as it rumbled below us. Tears stained my cheeks as I watched Valerie reach for his hand. Even if we could get him to a hospital there was no way they could save him. His chest seemed to shudder as he tried to say something to Valerie. Their eyes never left each other and she just shushed him.

"I know," she took a blood covered hand and held it to her chest. With the other hand she cupped his cheek. "I love you too."

"Would you be able to cauterize your own wounds?" I asked him.

Chauncy's eyes, dull with pain, lifted to mine as he shook his head and looked back at Valerie. He began to choke and blood streamed from the corner of his mouth.

"Don't leave me," Valerie held his hands and squeezed as if that would end his pain and bring him back from the brink. "Please."

Chauncy looked deep within her eyes and took one last shuddering breath before laying his head down for the last time. His eyes, which had just held the brightness that was Chauncy, were dull and lifeless now. A ripping surrounded my heart as Valerie began a keening that tore at my chest.

I looked up to see Moira smirking. She held Alexandar by the neck above the ground. His feet dangled lifelessly. I thought of Chauncy's laughter. I thought about how he held me while I cried and made me feel like I was worthy of being his friend. The first to hug and accept me. A dark and terrible rage broke inside me. She would not be allowed to take another of my friends.

An object dangling from her wrist caught my eye. It shone in the light around us, the shape familiar. My key warmed against my chest in response. It was another skeleton key. I drew my sword fully and knew my mark. Taking my stance, the wind blew hard within the room. I aimed for her wrist, attempting to cut free the chain that held the key.

I put my weight into the swing and to my pleasure hit my target. But I hit the target harder than I anticipated and cleaved her wrist from her arm. The key went flying. Before I could follow its flight Moira turned her sights on me, releasing Alexandar. There was anger but no visible pain that she had just lost a hand. I was defiant as she bared down on me. Alexandar moved slightly, just enough to trip her. It was enough of a distraction.

I crouched down and tried to pull Valerie away.

"We need to leave," I urged. "We have to regroup."

Valerie threw herself on top of Chauncy and began shaking.

"I'm not leaving him," she wailed.

"Oh gosh," came a now familiar voice. "Guess I still have some work to do."

I turned toward the sound to see that Moira had righted herself, with a foot heavily on her brother's windpipe. I stood to protect Valerie, still sobbing in her grief.

"You were right about one thing earlier," she looked at Alexandar on the ground.

"What's that?" I could feel a tornado baring its ugly teeth down on us and I was ready to take her out with me.

"He was in love with you," she chuckled, releasing her foot and kicking his body. He didn't move. "Though I'm not exactly sure what he saw in you."

My heart squeezed at her use of the past tense.

I moved into my now practiced crouch but Moira easily knocked the sword out of my hand this time. She wrapped her good hand around my neck and lifted. A black ooze was be seeping from the stump on her left arm.

"Don't," Moira warned. "Or I'll snap her neck."

I gripped Moira's hand, struggling to breathe. I heard the sword clatter to the ground. Her pale face seemed to glow in the low light. My shoulders hitched as I forced air into my lungs but there was no relief. I thought I saw a flash of white behind Moira, but that could have been my brain's reaction to the lack of oxygen. Moira's laughter was the last thing I heard before my vision dimmed completely.

I woke to an incessant clanging. My head was fuzzy and the inside of my mouth felt like someone had installed shag carpet. I struggled to sit up but my wrists and ankles were bound to a bed. My heart began to pound and I thrashed wildly calling for Alexandar, then Valerie, then Chauncy. Anyone who would answer. My body was on fire, but I fought the bindings harder.

The walls were covered in some kind of torn and stained padding. There was a single door that broke the four walls that surrounded me and a thin window that had reinforced bars. The stench of urine permeated the room and I hoped to all that was holy that it wasn't me. The mattress I lay on was thin and dimpled. I was wearing a hospital gown. I began screaming in earnest. Tears ran from my eyes and my voice became hoarse. The clanging had finally ceased and in the quiet I heard footsteps. Tears were flowing freely down my cheeks when I heard the jingle of keys in my doorway.

The door opened with a creak and three men with clip boards and lab coats entered the room.

"Subject 24563," one of them said. "Nineteen-year-old female, severe schizophrenia triggered by the trauma of her sister's tragic death. Committed by her mother."

"It says here she's never been lucid since she arrived. She has been on constant sedatives to counteract her rages when someone challenges her," another one stated.

As they spoke I looked desperately for any sign that I wasn't really here, that this wasn't my reality.

"That's right," the first nodded.

"Then why is she lucid right now?" The second asked.

"That's impossible," the first took a penlight from his coat pocket and shined it in my eyes. I blinked and tried to close my eyes at the brightness.

"Can I have some water?" I asked.

"Extraordinary," the first gaped at me. "Has her drug regimen changed?"

The third man flipped a couple of pages on the clipboard and shook his head to the negative. The first unbound my wrists and feet then handed me a cup of water. I gulped it greedily. My wrists itched and looked raw from the bindings. They bled lightly.

"Do you know where you are?" The second man was taking quick notes and asking me questions.

"No," I frowned. "Where are my friends?"

They looked at each other and nodded.

"Which friends?" The first asked.

"Alexandar, Chauncy and Valerie." I stated, though I was dreading the answer.

"We have no patients with those names at this facility," the second replied after flipping pages again.

"What facility?" I asked.

"Healing Hand Psychiatric Hospital," the first responded.

Though I'd just had some water my throat was dry again. It was difficult to swallow around the lump forming in my throat. Had it all been a drugged out haze? I had been given everything I'd ever wanted. Adventure, power, confidence, attraction and friends.

"None of it was real?" I was suddenly very tired.

"No," the first doctor said. "I'm sorry. We have more rounds to make but we will come back and talk some more."

He patted my knee encouragingly then left, locking the door behind him. I stared at my hands in my lap and then closed my eyes. I tried to find my Element. I tried to pick up the slack of the mystical link that bound me and my friends. Tried to find the anchor of the other Elementals. I came up empty. The loss of those things seemed a lot to bear at the moment, a heavy weight pressing against my chest. After a while I stood and wandered to the tiny window. My gown hung around me, wet with sweat, tears and blood.

Outside the window there was a lonely oak tree in a sea of crabgrass and weeds. I breathed deep as I watched the breeze blow through the weeds. There seemed to be a lot of dandelions surrounding my side of the building and I took comfort in that even if it wasn't real. I watched as the flowers began to seed. A breeze blew through them and lifted the tiny white fluffs into the air. There were so many that wind seemed to create a tangible cloud of seedlings.

I wasn't sure why but when I was finished watching the scene I felt better. When the doctors came back I smiled and made nice. I answered their questions. The third doctor never spoke a word through it all. I kept my eye on him while the other two spoke, that was the only reason I saw it when I did.

As they were leaving I caught a hint of shark teeth. After the other two had left he closed the door behind him and curled his scarred lip at me. I smiled back and waved. I would bide my time. I knew that they would come for me. I still had my faith and I would never lose sight of what was real.

Dear Reader,

Thank you so much for reading my book. I really hope you enjoyed reading it as much as I enjoyed writing it. Please leave me a review at your favorite retailer!

Yours Truly,

S.M. Winter

About the Author

S.M. Winter grew up in Des Moines, Washington. She loved reading the R.L. Stein: *Goosebumps* series when she was young and graduated to fantasy novels shortly thereafter. She has been writing since she was able to hold a pen. Two authors and screen writers who have inspired her most are Nora Robert aka J.D. Robb and Tina Fey.

S.M. Winter graduated from Central Washington University in 2009 with a Bachelor's degree in Theatre Arts. She spent most of the time behind the scenes, directing and writing scripts. Her favorite play is Cyrano De Bergerac which she played a part in high school and sent her on her path to Theatre Arts.

When she isn't writing, S.M. Winter spends most of her time working at a local Starbucks and spending time with her husband and three-year-old son. Binge-watching streaming television shows and movies is another favored past time.

Read S.M. Winter's writing tips and tricks at www.winterwarren.com .

Other Books by this Author

Look for Book Two in the Elemental Series, coming soon.

For updates please follow her blog: www.winterwarren.com .

Connect with S.M. Winter

Thank you so much for reading True North: Book One in the Elemental Series. Here are my social media coordinates:

Find me on Facebook: www.facebook.com/warrenofwinter
Follow me on Twitter: @warrenofwinter
Follow me on Instagram: @warrenofwinter
Favorite my Smashwords Author Page:
Subscribe to my blog/website: www.winterwarren.com

If you're interested in having your very own Elemental Key check out Aspiring ArtistA's shop: www.etsy.com/shop/aspiringartista

65102183R00104

Made in the USA
Lexington, KY
01 July 2017